Apache Gold

WANTED. MEN NOT AFRAID OF APACHES AS ESCORT ON VENTURE INTO MOUNTAINS. WAGES PLUS SHARES.

Hannibal Heyes passed the newsprint to Curry and said, 'Another lost mine dream.'

Eyes on the ceiling Chavez purred, 'Not a mine. A large quantity of gold. Not lost. There's a valid map. An adventure, gentlemen, to recover a fortune. For a beautiful boss lady. Doesn't that intrigue you?'

Heyes leaned forward. 'How big a party has she got so far? What will a share amount to?'

Chavez folded his arms on the desk and smiled. 'No takers yet whom I'd approve. Some shifty hyenas came sniffing around who'd cut a throat for a peso. We don't want that kind.'

'But you approach us?' Heyes was mocking. 'A pair wanted for bank and train robberies, worth ten thousand each? You think we'd bring the treasure back here?'

The mobile lips puckered, then Chavez said dreamily, 'You might. You might not. I don't really care. The money doesn't interest me.'

Also by Brian Fox in the 'Alias Smith & Jones' series, published in Tandem editions

DEAD RINGER
OUTLAW TRAIL
CABIN FEVER

Apache Gold

Brian Fox

First published in Great Britain by Tandem
Publishing Ltd, 1976

Tandem Books are published by Tandem Publishing Ltd,
14 Gloucester Road, London SW7
A Howard & Wyndham Company

Made and printed in Great Britain by
Hunt Barnard Printing Ltd., Aylesbury, Bucks.

Chapter One

Tucson was a far cry from the American cow towns, rail heads and mining camps Hannibal Heyes and his partner Jeb Kid Curry had roistered and ghosted through in their wide ranging prowling of the west on the outlaw trail. Almost without exception those were of sun-warped wood, grayed with weathering and dust, innocent of paint.

Tucson was different in both construction and population. Its origin was Spanish. It was made of mud. Of 'dobe and straw bricks, laid up and calcimined to prevent their melting in the rain. Square, squat houses washed with sky blue, yellow, shocking pink plaster that faded and flaked to expose the dun colored base. The effect on the eye was of bravura harlequin motley, a town fighting for its life against the elements. Like small forts the flat-topped buildings bristled with the stub ends of logs that supported the roofs, protruding from the walls, handy for hanging long loops of hot, red chilli peppers to dry and clay ollas in woven grass nets to cool water in the shade.

There was a forlorn gaiety, a day-after-the-fiesta droop almost tangible in the stifling air, a weary look that reflected submission by the inhabitants to the domination of political corruption. The Tucson Ring, a shadowy band of brokers whose power extended into the heart of territorial government, kept a stranglehold all along the border. Cynics joked that the Ring would steal the gold out of a man's mouth unless it was wired closed. Their wealth accumulated from dealings in contraband. Forbidden guns sold to Indians.

Rustled herds driven up from Mexico and sold to the army to feed the reservations. Whiskey for everyone, white and red man.

Where Heyes and Curry had cut a wide swath with years of daring and successful bank and train robberies and were prominently represented in most sheriffs' offices by WANTED posters, unrecognizable drawings made by artists from hysterical descriptions given by victims, but offering flattering rewards for their capture, the Ring operated even more flagrantly, serene in their immunity. Their brand of villainy was still secure and profitable. For Heyes and Curry, time had run out.

Hannibal Heyes had been one of the first of the hoot owls to read the future correctly. The web of telegraph wires being rapidly spun throughout the west made every day more hazardous for the knights of the road. Almost before any robbery was completed the alarm was sent winging and received in so broad an area that escape except by air was becoming all but impossible. No spider had more immediate communication with the most extreme perimeter of its trembling, sticky filaments.

When the Governor, harassed by overcrowded jails and clogged courts, had offered a pardon to wanted men who would apply and foreswear any further outlawry, Hannibal Heyes had seen a golden opportunity to quit the profession voluntarily before he and the Kid were gunned down by some trigger-happy posse or caught and locked up for the rest of their lives.

Lom Trevors who had ridden many a trail with them had seen the light long before Heyes, had turned himself around, moved to the side of the law and proved himself, won the position of Sheriff of Porterville. Hannibal Heyes shot down one after another of Kid Curry's arguments against giving up the life they had so long enjoyed, and when he had won his points they went to their old friend for a helping hand.

With their reputations, a pair at the top of every wanted list, a fortune in ransom on their heads, they could not present themselves in person to the Governor. It would be suicide to try to get within even telegraph distance of him.

They could send a wire, yes, but while they waited for an answer at a location they would have to specify a wolf pack of bounty hunters, law officers; men dazzled by the hope of collecting on them would howl down on them before a pardon could save them.

Trevors took more convincing than Kid Curry had. They loved the old ways too much to give them up, he said, they had too much fun in outwitting the law, the railroad police, the Pinkertons. Furthermore, he told the boys, the offer of pardon was directed at the petty criminals who did not cost their prey too much. It was not intended to extend to such luminaries as Hannibal Heyes and Jeb Kid Curry who had taken so heavy a toll of the treasures of major institutions.

Heyes caught at that as a drowning man at a broomstick. Those institutions would be better off, their money safer, if he and the Kid gave their word to do no more raiding in exchange for security and legal freedom. He had risen to leadership of the gangs he had ridden with by persuasion, not violence, and never had he put more heart into the art than in winning over Lom Trevors. Finally the sheriff had laughed, admitted that the boys sounded sincere and Heyes' reasoning was solid, and agreed to visit the capital and intercede for them.

He was gone a worrisome, suspicious length of time. Kid Curry gave up hope, wanted to ride out and not wait. If Lom had not succeeded, he complained, they were sitting ducks in Porterville where the infernal telegraph could bring an order for their arrest. Heyes agreed in part. They hid out in the hills and visited Trevors' living quarters behind his jail only in the small hours of the dark mornings.

Then Trevors was back, left a lamp in his window as a signal, and when the boys slipped through the door met them with heavy drinks already poured.

'Sit down and swallow fast. You're going to need both.'

A tall, broad, square-shouldered man, proud of his carriage, normally a friendly, outgoing, even-tempered person, Trevors looked and sounded tonight harried, impatient, put upon, defensive.

Hannibal Heyes threw the whiskey back, sank on the edge

of a chair, his stomach tightening, his voice empty.

'We don't get it?'

Kid Curry's glass shook in his hand. 'I knew it wouldn't work.'

Trevors said, 'You get it', and took his drink in a long, slow draught.

Heyes' brows climbed as high as they would go. 'Then why the face? You look like a pall bearer.'

'Feel like one.' The sheriff sighed from the bottom of his lungs. 'I got you an amnesty only, not a pardon yet, and I don't believe you'll ever make that. You're on probation for a year. Break a law, any law at all, and the whole thing's out the window.'

Suspicion crawled coldly up Heyes' spine. 'If we go straight we go straight, don't we? What are you holding out?'

'A kicker, boys,' Trevors leaned to fill the glasses again before he went on. 'I talked myself blue in the face. The Governor is scared of political backfire if he lets you off scot free. Same with the Attorney General. All I could get was a compromise. A year to see if you can behave. Twelve months while only those two and I know there's a deal hanging.'

'Oh.' Heyes felt as if he had been kicked in the head. 'For a year we have to eat, make a living doing something you'll accept, but stay on the dodge. Great.'

Trevors sounded unsure. 'You've never been caught yet.'

'We've never been clay pigeons either.'

'I know.' The sheriff scrubbed a hand through his thick hair. 'I don't see a glimmer that you can cut the conditions. There's the offer if you want to try. But,' he glared from Curry to Heyes, spread his big fingers flat on the table, 'I went out on the end of a limb for you. I've worked like hell to be able to hold my head up. I can look the Governor in the eye today. If you take on this year, and if you let me down, hurt my record, I'm coming after you with everything I've got. Others haven't been able to find you when they looked but both of you know that I can and will.

'You want to think it over for a day?'

Both Kid Curry and Hannibal Heyes were gamblers and good ones. Both also found an inner joy in danger and challenge. Heyes cocked a brow at the Kid, a familiar sparkle in his clear eyes.

'Go for broke, partner?'

Curry's nature was happy-go-lucky, carefree, and he seldom borrowed trouble. He offered a hand and Heyes shook it, then faced Trevors squarely again.

'We're in. And remember I've never broken my given word. There's one thing, Lom. If something comes up that's too much for us to handle inside the law can we come to you for advice?'

'Advice yes. A grubstake if you're against the wall. That's it'.

The months since that night had been lean. Honest money was elusive and hard work to make. The boys had gambled first and kept afloat until the poker game when Kid Curry had shot a cheating dealer in the hand. The hit was not accident. Curry was a better shot than anyone he had ever met, with any kind of gun. He had proved it many times and his reputation had spread far, helping to conceal a secret he and Heyes shared with Lom Trevors. Neither outlaw had ever killed a human being.

But that game had stopped their gambling as a new occupation to live by. There was too much likelihood of running into trouble in a saloon. They had withdrawn to the mountains, to remote places where there was less chance of being found by those who hunted them for the rewards still being offered, and panned gold from the streams. But being novices at mining they had been swindled out of their dust at one site and at another nearly trapped into bank robbery by a scheming Wells Fargo agent. Many trades were closed to them because they had no training in much aside from outlawry.

They had come to Tucson as drovers for a freighting company, had been paid off and gone to a cantina to relax after the gruelling days of skinning the obstinate mule teams across the desert. At a table there the Mexican behind the faro shoe had used a mirror ring that neither Heyes nor Curry discovered in the deft hand until they were down to two dollars, and when they called him the whole room drew against them. Aside from the Tucson Ring there was only a handful of gringos in the town and they were considered fair game by the Spanish blood locals.

Hannibal Heyes was not as fast as Curry but both their guns were out before any others. The dim room froze, the boys the center of a bristling circle. A carnage hung by the thread of a split second. Then surprisingly a rumble of laughter rolled from the rear and an easy voice speaking Spanish.

'Think twice, amigos. If any of you fire you will be dead before your bullet strikes either American. I know.'

There was movement from a far corner. The boys did not look, they were watching dark eyes for a twitch that would mean a tightening finger on a trigger. None came. Instead there was a slacking off from the dangerous instant. They heard footsteps, then the voice just behind them, using English now.

'Move slowly. I will walk you out of here.'

The partners turned with care. A man was there, sandy, unkempt, not impressive except for the confident smile on his soft, mobile lips. He stepped between them, touched their shoulders, pushing them backward firmly. They gave ground and the circle separated, let them through. Step by step they moved to the door, guns still in their hands, continuing to watch for a sign that someone would take a chance. No one did. The man pushed aside the bright serape that covered the low doorway, held it while the boys backed out, stood quietly where he blocked the entrance until they were out of the line of fire. Then he dropped the hanging and joined them on the unlighted street. A moon showed his face, still smiling.

'Gentlemen,' he said airily, 'these are excitable people, volatile, and they resent anyone from the north.'

Hannibal Heyes dropped his gun in the holster, awe on his damp face, in his tone. 'Just how did you manage that piece of magic? And many thanks.'

He had a soft chuckle. 'Not magic. I am half Mexican, and I am a personage. Emile Chavez, editor of the *Tucson Sun*, at your service.'

Kid Curry whistled without sound. In spite of the heat that was still as fiery as the day had been, sweat was chill against his back and his voice shook.

'Mr Chavez, I know a guardian angel when I see one. That was nice thinking, saying we're sharpshooters, buying time. It was quick.'

'You give me credit that isn't due.' The editor laughed quietly. 'I had been watching you, expecting you to spot Gonzalez' game earlier. I had understood you were both experts at gambling as well as other crafts.'

'Huh?' Curry was shocked. 'You know us?'

'Of course. Once I interviewed a banker, was present while you relieved his establishment. Even without the masks your eyes are distinctive.'

'Oh no. Mr Chavez, we're in your debt, but not so much that we'll go quietly along to a jail. We . . .'

'Farthest thing from my mind, boys. How nearly did Gonzalez clean you out?'

'All but,' Hannibal Heyes told him sheepishly.

The editor linked his hands through their arms and began walking, saying, 'Perhaps I can help. Would you be interested in a job? It's honest and it's dangerous, but it could pay well. Come to the office and I'll show you an ad, tell you what I know.'

Chapter Two

Emile Chavez unlocked the door of a single story mud building that had been altered, a hole knocked in the front wall and a window installed. It was the only window Heyes and Curry had seen on a street front. In the old Spanish fashion properties were closed away from public view, houses and shops constructed around a patio where shade trees, geraniums, hardy shrubs and flowers that needed no watering were cultivated and tables, chairs under the trees invited langor. In that hot, burned up land no one exerted himself more than was absolutely necessary.

The editor entered an archway the depth of a room, opened another door on the left side of the passage and left the boys outside until he had put a match to a lamp with a green glass shade hanging over a littered desk. Then he invited them in, flicking a hand toward rough built chairs with cowhide seats and backs, and took one similar on the far side of the desk. He pawed through sheets of paper covered with script as fine and precise as copper plate engraving, uncovered a single fold newspaper, laid it before Heyes, pointing to a small boxed notice, then leaned back, rocking on the rear legs of the chair, clasping his hands behind his large head, smiling at the ceiling.

The make-up of the paper was not American. The front page carried the advertising, logically, Heyes thought, since that was what paid for publication. The type in the ad was chosen from different fonts with little concern for upper or lower case. It made reading difficult but set against the regularity of the rest of the page it was eye catching.

WANTED. MEN NOT AFRAID OF APACHES AS ESCORT ON VENTURE INTO MOUNTAINS. WAGES PLUS SHARES.

Hannibal Heyes passed the newsprint to Curry and said in disappointment, 'Another lost mine dream. If you live long enough to get old and feeble running after those will-o-the-wisps.'

Chavez did not comment until Curry held the paper over the desk, opened his thumb and finger and let it waver down to the desk, disdain in the gesture.

Eyes still on the ceiling Chavez purred, 'Not a mine. A large quantity of gold already extracted. Not lost. There's a valid map. An adventure, gentlemen, to recover a fortune. For a beautiful boss lady. Doesn't that intrigue you?'

Heyes leaned forward to read the date at the top of the page. It was a week old. A corner of his mouth tipped up.

'How big a party has she got so far? What will a share amount to in a split?'

Chavez squared his chair on the floor, folded his arms on the desk and smiled at Heyes, at Curry, purring again.

'No takers yet whom I'd approve. Some shifty hyenas came sniffing around who'd cut a throat for a peso. We don't want that kind.'

'But you approach us?' Heyes was mocking. 'A pair wanted for bank and train robberies, worth ten thousand each? You think we'd bring a treasure back here?'

The mobile lips puckered into a red O, then Chavez said dreamily, 'You might. You might not. I don't really care. The money doesn't interest me.' At Curry's snort of derision the editor chuckled softly, a secret sound of enjoying a private joke. 'I know you find that doubtful, but every man to his own last. I am an editor. A writer. I have a paper to fill with copy and that requires stories. People don't buy the *Sun* to read advertisements, they buy it for gossip, news, excitement. This can be one whale of a story. It can be a whole series of chapters. It can double circulation and keep it booming week after week.

'As to why I make the proposition to you boys, I have followed your exploits through the press and sketchy as the reports have been one thing shines through all of them. One or both of you is or are extraordinarily adept at making a strike, vanishing with your loot, over and over again. In other words you know how to survive in a hostile society. Kid Curry's gun is a legend. Further, I have never read of your harming passengers on the trains you stopped nor of any brutalities against bank employees. There appears to be a gallantry in your operations that suggests a high intelligence not commonly credited to outlaws.

'Tell me what better qualities I could look for in men to ride into Apache country with.'

Kid Curry stood up, placed his hat, that had a hole worn at the pinched front of the crown, over his heart and made a ceremonious bow toward Heyes, working to keep his face straight, and Heyes had the grace to flush. He was not accustomed to such gratuitous compliments from men, although women often flattered him. He looked at the editor more closely.

Emile Chavez appeared a retiring, unaggressive man who would bend in the winds of events rather than break. He would not be noticed in a crowd. But the sandy lashes were thick and long, screening the eyes behind them. Hannibal Heyes could not read the expression but he had an impression that he and Curry were under a microscope, were in some way being played with. It was an uncomfortable sensation while not being aggravating. The thought struck him that the front window had been cut so Chavez could watch whatever went on outside, indicating a fertile curiosity.

Thinking aloud Heyes said, 'I guess we haven't anything else in sight right away and we could use some wages. If you're willing to trust your judgement of us, all right. It will be something new for us.'

'The challenge. Yes, I thought that would tempt you.' Chavez sounded pleased with his good guess.

'The boss lady, will we meet her before we leave?' Kid Curry was always interested in women, especially the beautiful as the editor had described this one.

'Oh my yes, tomorrow morning.' There was light laughter under the words. 'I had better know how to introduce you. I assume you're not using your notorious names?'

Curry jabbed a thumb against his chest, his lips quirking. 'I'm Thaddeus Jones. He's Joshua Smith. They don't attract much attention.' He stood up, stretching his waist to finger the two Mexican dollars in his pocket, enough for a hotel room and a breakfast, and with a job ahead he did not worry. 'Where do we meet you?'

'At the Alvarado Hotel, but just a minute.' Chavez unlocked a lower drawer, brought up a cash box and fanned ten bills before them, a hundred dollars. 'An advance to do some outfitting for perhaps a two-week ride. We will take care of animals and supplies. If that is satisfactory, good evening, friends.'

Hannibal Heyes folded the money, put it away, shook the hand Chavez offered and they left, Heyes feeling his face stiffen with chagrin. A hundred dollar advance was a lot and he understood exactly why. This unpretentious editor was a long way from as innocent and open as he posed. The hundred was a test, insurance, and a lot less to lose if his hired escort simply pocketed it and left town between suns than it could cost if they doublecrossed him on the trail. They were being put on their mettle in a subtle fashion. On the way to the hotel he had to explain the maneuver to the Kid. Curry was walking on air at the apparent generosity of the writer-editor, with his head in the clouds. It made Curry mad to have been taken in but he could never stay mad for long and after a celebrating drink at the hotel bar he stretched out in the room on the first bed either had had for too long to lay grinning in the dark, making guesses about the woman they would work for.

None of the guesses matched the reality when the boys went down the single flight of steps in the morning. The Alvarado was one of the few two story buildings in Tucson, wrapped around an inner court, the rooms opening on a wide balcony, railed by iron scrollwork. From the top Heyes and Curry saw Emile Chavez come through the street gate, cross the court, and met him at the bottom. In daylight his skin was fair with an indoor softness, letting his bland features change without the furrows of sun wrinkles.

He showed no surprise at seeing the pair still in town, nodded a greeting and beckoned them with him through the lobby entrance, saying, 'We'll join Miss Christian, Angela Christian, in the dining room. She should be breakfasting about now.'

The room was spacious, dim, the hot sun kept out by 'dobe walls three feet thick, the only light filtered through deeply recessed narrow windows. There were men at some of the tables covered with snowy Spanish linen, some of them drummers to judge by their dress, others dark skinned, their origin obvious. Neither Hannibal Heyes nor Kid Curry saw any of them. They saw only the single female figure present, seated alone beneath a window facing them. A shaft of early morning light glinted in hair so pale it shone like a halo of fine mist above a slender oval face. Chavez made a pleased sound, heading for her, and following Heyes and Curry discovered that her mouth was richly curved, her nose thin walled, straight from her forehead with no depression of the bone, the nostrils slanted up and outward in a proud flare. Her brows matched her hair, too pale to show, making an exotic impression. Her lids spread like a bird's wings from a fold at the inner corners, up and outward. The eyes beneath them were intense, so deep a blue as to verge on purple. She did not smile as the three men approached but sat stiffly as if under tension.

The editor of the *Tucson Sun* swept off his wide brimmed, flat hat, saying in concern, 'Miss Christian my dear, is something troubling you this morning?'

She barely glanced at Heyes and Curry, fastening her attention on Chavez. Her voice was low, musical but strained.

'My father did not come in last night. No stage came in.'

'And you are afraid it was stopped, perhaps by Indians?' There was indulgent humor in the tone. 'You should not worry. Not until definite news comes through. There can be many reasons for a delay. Now see who I have brought you, two gentlemen most eminently qualified for our adventure. Joshua Smith on the left, Thaddeus Jones on the right. Gentlemen, Miss Angela Christian.'

Without asking her permission Emile Chavez took the chair at her side and waved the boys to those opposite. Curry sank into his with an audible sigh of admiration, unable to take his eyes off the vision across from him. A pulse in Hannibal Heyes' temple throbbed but he reined in his automatic enthusiasm, remembering that not so long ago another beauty had so deceived them that she had all but got them killed. This time he would hold his judgement in cold reserve.

The disturbing eyes were looking at him now, and at Curry, liking what they saw if the relaxation of the face was any indication. Chavez allowed time for the survey by all three, let their first reactions settle in, then spoke quietly, nudging them on, suggesting that Miss Christian tell the escort in her own words what the proposed trip was about.

She had been living in St Louis with her widowed father. His brother, her uncle, had spent years prospecting all through this country, had found a rich vein in the Superstitions and mined out a lot of nearly pure metal. He had come out of the mountains and sent a map and a letter to her father, Burt Christian, with a generous offer.

Mining, Uncle Avery wrote, was boring to him, it was the search for mineral, the finding of it that was important to him. Therefore he had hidden the gold because he felt his brother needed to get out of his period of mourning his wife and thought a new goal with some excitement to reach it would interest him in life again. If Burt would go into the mountains and bring out the fortune waiting there Avery was giving it to his brother and niece in equal shares while he himself went looking for another strike.

Her father had taken the map and prepared for the trip but Angela had insisted on going along. Burt Christian had led a mysterious life, vanishing from home sometimes for months at a time and returning with no explanation of where he had been or what he had done, until his wife's death six months before. She did not trust him to bring her legacy to her.

He had agreed readily. She should go west alone, arrange for a party sufficient to withstand Indians to go with them while he put their eastern affairs in order, and wait for him in Tucson. He was now two full days late and she trusted him even less. She was not so afraid his stage had met with foul play as that he had not intended coming here but was headed into the Superstitions by another route to cut her out of her share of the gift.

Hannibal Heyes and Kid Curry felt an immediate kinship with the prospecting uncle. Their own experiences had proved that mining was not only boring but very hard work. Whatever the wages would be for their part in the recovery, it would be very satisfying to share in the result of someone else's toil with pick and shovel.

'There's only one drawback,' Heyes said reluctantly. 'Thad and I don't know the Superstitions and they have a bad reputation. The worst kind of country and the Apaches think it's all theirs.'

'No problems there,' Chavez flicked a hand across the tablecloth. 'There'll be a guide who knows his way and the Indians won't be up there now. This time of year when a bunch of broncos jump the reservation to go raiding they go north where it's cooler . . . Here's the guide now. I told him eight o'clock to give us an opportunity of talking first.'

The editor rose, extending a hand to the man who crossed the dining room. He was an imposing figure, tall, built with the hard thickness of a lion but looking slender, carrying himself like a coiled spring, with a fluid balance. Handsome, the planes of his face sharply carved, his hair blue black and straight, there was a hint of Indian about him except in the cold light green blue of his long, narrow, restless eyes.

'Ross Eaton,' Chavez said and made introductions.

Eaton offered no handshake except to Chavez, covering the lapse by turning to wheel another chair to the end of the table. He barely glanced at Heyes and Curry, like them focusing only on the singular girl, his rather thin mouth spreading in a straight smile that showed the mere tips of white, strong teeth. His voice when he spoke held a controlled resonance.

'Miss Christian, the morning stage pulled in as I reached the hotel. Several men got off, possibly one is your father.'

The girl looked quickly through the archway into the lobby as a flurry of arrivals made a commotion. The clerk at the desk answered a question asked by a short, slight man who dropped a carpet bag on the tile floor and came through the arch with a rolling, gimpy step, hurrying. Seen from the front he was wizened, his hair ragged, nondescript above a small face webbed with many sharp but shallow wrinkles, the look of one who has used himself hard most of his life. Behind him two other men followed, lagging back, one taller than average, lean as a cadaver, tanned to a dark leather color with a taciturn expression, the other short, square, a bulldog.

Angela Christian made a low sound, a moan of relief, and waved her napkin in a signal that was not necessary. The little man was making a bee line for the table. He hopped behind Chavez to peck a kiss on the girl's forehead as she lifted her face, and pat her shoulder.

'Finally got here, honey. Did you about give up on me? What happened was, after I left St Louis I got a brainstorm. Avery used to team up sometimes with some other boys and

I'd met a couple. It seemed to me if I could bring them in we'd be better off with some help I was sure knew what they were about. No offense to whoever you hired on. So meet Eddie Brown and Bob Kenny. They're rarin' to go for just a little cut, mostly for the fun of being out on a trail. Who all you got here?'

Introductions went around again, Heyes and Curry all at once trying to make themselves invisible as surprise piled on suspicion. Again Chavez orchestrated the planning, then the guide Eaton left to arrange for horses, a string of pack burros to haul in foodstuffs and camping gear and bring out the gold in bags they would take with them. There was no reason, all agreed, that they should not leave after a noon meal, get half a day's jump on the track. Burt Christian had showed his map to Eaton who said he knew the canyons that would best take them to Avery's site, a cave high on the precipitous flank of the mountain.

Christian and his men went to change from traveling dress to rugged clothes and took the girl with them to outfit her more suitably. Heyes and Curry were left at the table with Chavez, neither wanting to call attention to himself by moving while the others were there. The editor was rising to leave when the partners found a common voice, one of disbelief.

'Miss Christian, she's not really going, is she?'

Chavez sank back. 'She is. To look as feminine as she does she has a steel trap determination. You heard her say she doesn't trust her father and having seen him I understand. He looks a bit shifty to me.'

Kid Curry exploded. 'It's too dangerous. She could be hurt. She'd give out. That's no place for a . . . a . . . '

'Fragile child of the city? Don't underestimate any woman where a fortune is involved. They are amazing creatures. Survival has been their profession since time began. The party is large enough to take care of her. I'll leave you now to buy what clothes and ammunition you'll want and meet you after dinner at the livery. There'll be two weeks' wages at the bank waiting when we get back.' Chavez got up without hurry and sauntered off, whistling a tune behind his teeth.

Heyes and Curry sat where they were, isolated now that

the breakfast crowd had melted away.

'I need a drink,' the Kid said in a hollow tone.

Heyes signaled a Mexican waitress for more coffee and whiskey to lace it, saying nothing more until the girl had brought the order and gone, simply looking into Curry's dark eyes. Then he filled his lungs.

'Cop. It's all over him. Didn't he know us? Or what's he up to?' Ross Eaton's big presence loomed in Heyes' mind.

Curry was staring back, looking haunted. 'And that pair with Christian. Their pictures are plastered around this country too. Highwaymen. Stages carrying treasure boxes their specialty. Hannibal, what are we into anyhow?'

Heyes swallowed from the warm drink. 'We aren't in. The thing for us to do is get on a horse and put all the distance we can between us and Tucson. Now.'

Curry yelped. 'You're crazy. Leave that girl in those claws? She'd be torn to pieces by Brown and Kenny. That banty father must be nuts to trust them, unless like she thought he wants her shut out of her cut and doesn't care what happens to her. Eaton. If they ganged up on him he couldn't protect her. We've got to go.'

Hannibal Heyes frowned, staring into his cup as if he could read the future in the grounds at the bottom.

'Eaton. I'd give something to know why he sat at this table with four wanted men and never batted an eye.'

'Maybe his badge and salary don't look so big against a shot at a fortune. We've known some law men with their hands out. This wouldn't be a much longer step than a bribe to look the other way.'

'I'd say no. He doesn't smell that way to me. He's got me curious.'

Curry sat back, tossed off his coffee and his lips quirked in a half smile. 'Me too. So let's find out. Brown and Kenny don't scare me and we've outsmarted all the law we've run into so far. It's something to do besides grow calluses sawing at a mule train or bucking a shovel, and we'll come out with a stake. There's nothing to spend money on where we'll be for two weeks or more.'

Hannibal Heyes still hesitated, but mysteries always made

him want to solve them and at length this one outweighed his caution. Kid Curry was right that they had come through all the tight places until now. He stood up, tugged on his hat and tapped it to a comfortable fit.

'You never git no honey unless you take a chance on gettin' stung,' he quoted an old saying chalked on a slate held by a cross-eyed girl named Ophelia, a newspaper cartoon that had given him a chuckle.

They bought new shirts and trousers, tough whipcord pants and wool shirts that would act as evaporators, keep them cooler than a lighter fabric. They bought a second short gun each. Chavez might arily dismiss Indians but Apaches might not behave according to his rules, and if they were jumped that was one type man they would feel permitted, even obliged to shoot.

They ate chilli and beans at a cantina rather than join the others at the hotel where Ross Eaton might have decided to make whatever play he had in mind. Then, warily, they approached the livery.

Chapter Three

Ross Eaton was in a quandary.

A year earlier a Wells Fargo Express stage carrying a green treasure chest loaded with minted gold coin and making a run through the southern desert where there was as yet no railroad had not come into the station. When it was a day overdue the route was tracked back. The big bright vehicle lay overturned at the side of the road. The team was gone, the driver riddled with bullets and scalped. There was no sign of the chest. To the investigators that fact ruled out Indian attack although the location was close to the Superstitions. Apaches were not interested in hauling around the heavy metal.

The tracks of three riders on unshod ponies driving the heavy team of four coach horses led away from the scene. Following, half a day later a campfire was found, cold ashes. Wet. There had been heavy rain in the night and the tracks were washed out from there.

The chest was not there but a soggy envelope tramped into the damp sand by a hoof, almost buried, caught the sharp eye of one of the search party. When it was carefully brushed an address could be made out. To an Avery Christian in care of the Tucson post office, from an Angela Christian with a number on Kings Highway, St Louis, Missouri.

With that clue to the robber murderers a watch had been established in Tucson for Avery Christian coming to pick up other mail. Ross Eaton knew him by sight, a big man with the look of the con artist who occasionally drifted through town, but he had seen no warrants out for him. Neither did anyone see Christian after the robbery. Another watch was put on the St Louis post office to look for letters sent to the Christian home there. When one arrived addressed to Angela and Burt Christian, bearing an Arizona postmark, the detective wanted to open it but the postmaster would not permit that. It was delivered intact and a stakeout put on the house. Shortly afterward Angelo booked a passage to Tucson and next day Burt left for Tombstone.

The Tombstone agent and Ross Eaton were alerted. The girl arrived in Tucson a week later and a courier brought Eaton word that Burt was on a stage coming north.

Eaton specialized in southwest and central Arizona. The district was pocked with mines and outlaws abounded there but were gradually being run down. In his four years in the territory Eaton had tracked several into the Superstitions, a favorite hideout, and now he knew much about the trails, scattered springs, tortuous deep dark canyons and precipitous mountain heights.

As a cover he dealt faro in a cantina, a choice place to hear rumor and pick up information, and there Emile Chavez visited him bringing a proof sheet of the *Sun* carrying Angela Christian's ad. They were close, as near friends as a good law officer and a canny editor allowed themselves. They put together the plan to join Burt Christian in his recovery project. Both wished for a larger group for protection in the mountains but neither found anyone they trusted. When Chavez enlisted Hannibal Heyes and Kid Curry, Ross Eaton was delighted at the irony. Technically he should turn the pair over to the local authority immediately, but they could be too useful in bringing out the gold. It would be dangerous. He would have to be on guard at all times, particularly after the chest was located when they could be expected to try to grab it themselves, but he thought he and Chavez could handle them and bring them to justice later.

Now there were complications. When Chavez had told him Angela's story Eaton had assumed she and her father were gullible victims of Avery, that for some reason he and his partners in the stage tragedy did not dare go into the mountains themselves and were using cat's paws. If his relatives succeeded in bringing out the treasure Avery would double-cross them. But here was Burt Christian turning up with two of Avery's partners, wanted as highwaymen. Was Burt in on a plot?

Two certain criminals and one unknown quantity added to Heyes and Curry stacked the odds considerably against Eaton. Worse, the girl was adamant about riding along. No argument of his had dissuaded her and Chavez had unaccountably, perversely taken her side. It was the wily editor's sense of humor and sense of story, Eaton knew, but that did not help matters. Lovely as she was, she too could be part of the conspiracy.

The Wells Fargo agent could not back out, be derelict in his duty, and there was nowhere to turn for help. The Tucson Ring had invisible tentacles everyplace and with the fortune at stake anyone he appealed to could be working for them.

He paced the livery waiting for the unsavory group to gather, made one last attempt to turn the blonde girl back when she appeared tricked out in pants and boots, even a little gun at her belt as if she thought the trip would be a picnic holiday. She was going and that was that.

Heyes and Curry were the last to arrive and Eaton knew at once by their quiet, surreptitious watchfulness that they at least suspected his role. It made his skin crawl, gave him a sense of nakedness. But so far Christian and his recruits appeared to take him at face value.

They got under way after one o'clock. There was little choice between riding at night or through the day, since the desert stored heat here and did not cool after sundown. Eaton took the lead with Angela at his side. She would not eat dust there and perhaps if he were adroit he could draw some truth out of her. But Emile Chavez scotched that for the time by pulling up abreast next to the girl.

Her father, Brown and Kenny rode single file to keep the burro string moving and Heyes and Curry withdrew to the drag.

Curry's eyes were narrow in the shade of his wide hat brim, boring against the broad, straight back ahead. In a low tone he mused, 'Is Eaton as stupid as he acts or has he got one hell of a lot of guts? Or is he just a crooked cop. Why is he here? Has the girl got him hypnotized?'

'I hope it's that.' Heyes was earnest. 'But something smells. There's a feeling in my bones that we're being conned to a fare-you-well. Either my brains are being broiled or there's something about this set-up that isn't the way we heard. Avery for instance. How long would he have to stay up there digging and sorting value out of county rock to collect what they say is a fortune? A year or more, by what we've seen of mining. Would the Apaches leave him alone all that time making holes in their territory? I don't believe it. They'd come down on him and he'd never know what hit him.

'But the cop believes there's something up there worth taking big risks to get at. It's easier for me to think Avery stole money and stashed it and couldn't go back for it. That way this burst of generosity makes more sense. If he could get somebody he trusted to run this errand for him he could contact his brother later and maybe draw a share.'

'Uh-huh. Eaton could be Wells Fargo going for the money. If he is he knows who we are and he knows those two amateur road agents. Hannibal, if that's all so, you've got to admire the man or call him a fool, riding out here with at least four of us *desperados* and no back-up. He can get himself killed by those two bit bums. Be a switch, wouldn't it, if we had to side him?'

'It might come to that, Kid. It'll be interesting to watch.'

The afternoon grew hotter with a bone-dry wind like a blast furnace. They did not push the pace and Eaton warned to use the least water they could get along on. It would be midnight, twenty miles before they could dig into a dry arroyo to an underground seep.

Angela required more than the men, keeping a damp handkerchief pressed against her lips, a thin-skinned city girl whose body lost moisture more rapidly than the men whose suntans helped conserve their fluids.

After sundown when the sky and air went through a dazzling series of color changes from gold through crimson, magenta, mauve to deepening blue of advancing dark, Eaton called a halt for a cold supper and a rest for the animals. Another twenty miles to the northeast the Superstition range rose in jagged peaks to a crest like a crosscut saw. Lower they were fenced by thousand foot high organ-pipe stone pillars, the whole mass throwing back the sunset as if it were afire. It still blazed when the low desert dulled in shadow, a beckoning light, a challenge and a threat.

The party chewed cold tortillas rolled into cones and scooped full of chilli with beans and meat, cold to the touch, fiery in the mouth. Angela tasted the mix, could not eat it and took only the tough corn meal, leather-textured, leather-thin cakes, washing them down with the last swallows from her canteen. Then they rode again.

Heyes and Curry talked about sharing the little water they had left with the girl as the miles stretched on and thirst grew again. Not except as a last resort, they decided. Ross Eaton had taken her over and the farther they could keep from a tangle with him the better.

By the middle of the night she was asleep in her saddle, Eaton supporting her with a hand around one limp arm, Emile Chavez holding the other. She did not wake when the train halted on the lip of a streambed twenty feet above the rock strewn floor. Eaton got down, lifted her off the horse, and when Chavez had shaken out a blanket, laid her on that, protecting her from the short spiny weed clumps growing in the sand.

The men took turns with a shovel digging down through the bottom rocks, found dampness at five feet and a sluggish brown flow at ten, then climbed the steep bank to wait for the hole to fill and clear. The animals smelled water and had to be picketed solidly to prevent their crowding toward it. Though they could not have reached down to the rising level they could injure themselves or be trapped by a sudden rushing wall of flood if there was rain at the head of the arroyo.

The party slept and by daylight there was water enough to strain through a bandana, fill the canteens, make coffee and bring canvas buckets up to the horses and burros. They ate, saddled, loaded the pack animals and rode north up the slowly lifting land. At noon they stopped where sparse bunch grass grew on the bench, let the animals graze for an hour to conserve the feed they carried with them, and by evening were at the portal of a canyon winding into the foothills. There they camped for the night. Those mountains should not be entered after dark. The trails were narrow, steep, and where passage had been possible on a previous trip might be blocked by landslide, or a shelf one followed could have caved, leaving a sheer drop into an abyss.

A seep from some higher source made a damp path between two of the monolithic pallisade obelisks that guarded the entrance. Carved by eons of wind and rain most of these were still attached to the mountain bulk but this pair and others stood free, towering toward the sky, some capped with remnants of a harder strata, thick, flat stone that overhung the supporting columns, others worn to serrated needle points, rising out of rubble of the fallen slabs.

They ate before the sun went down, digging another water hole, this one just below the surface of the sloping ground that was littered with stones tumbled round by passage from the heights, washed down in flash floods. The brilliant rays off the western horizon were like a force that pinned every living thing against the fiery wall.

Angela Christian craned her head far back to look up the pillars, telling Emile Chavez in an awed tone, 'I don't wonder these mountains are called the Superstitions. They're eerie. So silent. It feels as though they're keeping awful secrets, that they're haunted by spirits. There's nothing friendly here as there is about the Ozarks. Are you sure it's safe to go in?'

The editor smiled, his long light lashes hiding a mischief lively in his eyes. 'Nothing is ever certain, Angela, that's why this is called adventure. Do you want to go back?'

'No.' The tone was positive. 'I'll get used to it. After all, they're only rock, they're not alive.'

'Why don't you ask Smith and Jones to take you for a walk, stretch your legs, look for signs of the things that do live here. You might find a rattlesnake they can shoot. The meat is a real delicacy. One would make a fine breakfast.'

He chuckled at her shudder and was pleased to see her glance toward Heyes and Curry, standing apart and watching her, then walk to them, saying loud enough that he could hear,

'That Mr Chavez is deliberately trying to frighten me. Now he tells me this isn't as safe as he said before and he wants us to kill a snake to eat. He's joking, isn't he?'

Across the ten feet that separated them Hannibal Heyes saw Chavez drop one eyelid closed without the other twitching and knew the girl was right. The man was playing a game, trying to draw a reaction, treating her like a puppet, perhaps to stir up a friction that would titillate the readers of his paper. Heyes swore at him silently. Friction they did not need with so many risks in such delicate balance. He had not considered the newsman a threat before but from here on he would bear serious consideration.

Recklessly Kid Curry touched the girl's arm, grinning, beckoning her with him and pointing at the right hand pillar, saying lightly, 'Maybe we can find him one back there. They really are good.'

She swallowed a lump in her throat, then to prove to herself that she was not going to let herself be ridiculed she headed up the grade at Curry's side. Heyes had tried to catch his partner's eye to warn him to let her strictly alone but he was too late. Their backs were already turned.

Across the camp Ross Eaton watched them leave, stood up from where he was crouched at the fire and angled after them without haste. Giving the blonde the benefit of his doubt about her involvement he meant to keep Kid Curry at a distance from her. He had already debated warning her about all four outlaws and discarded the idea. There were problems enough to juggle without risking that she was guilty and would report his charge or, if innocent would rashly challenge their intentions. Either way it could precipitate some action against him. He could be killed in his sleep and left while the rest went on. All he could do was to watch that none of them harmed her.

They were out of sight for some moments before Eaton got behind the pillar and saw them standing close together, hand in hand, looking up the canyon slope, Curry's right arm extended, pointing. Curry's move made Eaton blink. The arm struck down and in the space of the blink a gun was in the hand as the Kid came half around. Eaton's breath sucked in. He froze, as good as dead. The gun bucked, exploding, but not aimed at him. He heard the lead strike rock fifteen feet upgrade from him, looked that way and saw the whipping writhing of a sidewinder, its head blown off.

Angela Christian's scream was short, sharp, of surprise, not fear, cut off by her hand slapped against her mouth. Curry's gun flipped back into the holster as quickly as it had been drawn and he took her shoulders with a light shake, laughing.

'Sorry to startle you, ma'am, but those things have a mean bite. We can go ahead now.'

'No.' Ross Eaton's voice hit hard. 'There'll be more snakes out now the sun's gone and the light's getting bad. Come back to camp, Angela.'

He had barely finished speaking when the rest of the party boiled around the obelisk, guns drawn, no one knowing what the shot had meant, a fight or murder. Eaton kept his eyes on Curry and the girl but flapped a hand at the flailing coils, then stepped to Angela's side, took her arm and drew her down the grade. Kid Curry stiffened in offense, then realized the danger of calling Eaton at this time and walked to Heyes, his lip curled in mockery.

'A touch of sun, partner? You're a mite white.'

Heyes let out a slow sighing breath. 'A grandstand play. Did you think she knows enough about a fast draw to appreciate it?' His words were low, for Curry only.

The Kid matched the tone. 'I heard Eaton behind me and didn't want a shot in my back. The snake just came in handy, and now that cop will have second thoughts if he decides to throw down on me. A little insurance isn't a bad thing . . . You know something? All at once I'm bushed. I could go to sleep standing here.'

'Me too.' Heyes sounded surprised. 'A scare can burn up energy in a hurry.'

They took their blankets away from the others and upwind from the animals, rolling in them at once, noticing that everyone else was also bedding down. Apparently after the long hot day's ride the shock of Curry's shot had affected them too. Both boys dropped off as if they had been slugged.

A stab of sunlight from the crest of the range hit Hannibal Heyes' eyes and woke him abruptly. He had slept very late and sat up sharply, looking about with a quick shake of his head. Pain knifed through his skull. His mouth was stuffed with flannel. In a flash he knew that something was very wrong. The camp was not stirring. Kid Curry lay on his stomach snoring lightly. The party was scattered over a hundred square feet, quiet in sleep. Heyes picked them out one after another. Angela Christian curled up near her father's spidery shape. Ross Eaton close to them. The sandy editor beyond them at a distance. He looked for the two highwaymen, did not see them and swung in the direction of the picketed animals. Two horses and two burros were missing. He got up, jumped to Curry and prodded him with a boot. The Kid opened his eyes, wincing as if his head hurt too.

'Mister Jones,' Heyes said in a silky purr, 'we have been taken again. By a pair of the scrub of our old profession. Did that coffee last night taste right to you?'

'Huh?' Curry rolled to his knees. 'Taken how?'

'Avery Christian's partners are gone. So is part of the string.'

'What? Why?'

Curry's shout woke the sleepers. He got to his feet and they jogged to the girl and her father, Ross Eaton rising to face them, scowling. Heyes ignored him, stopping above Christian and pointing toward the animals.

'Your friends didn't wait for us today and I'd say they doped the coffee so we'd sleep through their packing. Have you still got your map or is it gone too?'

The man stared, stupid for a moment, scrambled to his feet, yanked out his shirt-tail and probed into a pocket of a money belt around his waist, sighed in relief and brought out a folded paper almost transparent with sweat grease. The rest gathered around as he opened it, holding it forward.

'It's here all right. Maybe they just went out of sight to . . . well . . . Maybe the animals tore loose and we'll find them close . . . '

'Saddled and loaded themselves? There's gear and grub missing.'

Emile Chavez stood back, a whimsical smile playing on his mouth, studying each of the party, in good humor. Ross Eaton stepped forward, took the map, looked at it closely and handed it back.

'Yes, this is the one you showed me in Tucson. I don't understand.'

Angela Christian reached for the paper, held it in both hands following the twisting lines drawn on it, then the hands began to tremble increasingly. Her voice too was unsteady.'

'Father, this is not the map Uncle Avery sent us.'

'Sure it is, honey. I never let go of it except to show the boys and you folks. And I watched it every minute then.'

'No. The map we had in St Louis was different.' She sat down on a large rock, spread the paper on her knees and traced the trail with a finger. 'Here. Up in the mountains where there's a branch and one way goes on but the other stops. This one makes a right turn. The other went left.

There were other guides and reference points that aren't the same as these. I remember some of them but not all.'

Curry started to speak but Heyes nudged him to keep out of the talk, let the girl and her father argue. But Ross Eaton had a question.

'Angela, drugged or not I think your father would have waked if Brown and Kenny had gotten into that belt to make a switch last night. Didn't you look at this drawing in Tucson?'

She raised wide, dark eyes with swollen pupils. 'No I didn't.' She swung on the little man. 'Burt Christian, what kind of trick are you trying? Did you send those men ahead with the true map to cheat me?'

Hannibal Heyes and Kid Curry knew from the drained face that Christian had not.

'Baby,' the man sounded strangled. 'I couldn't do that to you, you're my little girl.'

'Then where is it? They must have it. How did they get it?'

Christian's eyes turned sick, guilty, defeated, then vacant as they looked back in time and the pallor changed to crimson. His words came choked.

'On the stage from Tombstone. We were celebrating the gold we'd have. I guess I had a bit too much and went to sleep. We were up on top alone behind the jehu and when I came to they'd laid me on the roof so I wouldn't fall off. They could have made this up in Tombstone and got me drunk deliberately.'

Embarrassingly he began to weep, large salt tears that made rivulets through his wrinkles, sank onto the rock and wrapped his hands around his head between his knees.

Chapter Four

The war chief Chato was all Apache. Some of his bronco band had blood from Mexican mothers who had been captured and held as slaves, but his strain was pure, going back into the distant cloudy beginnings of The People.

That was how *Apache* translated, The People, the chosen. A tribe of barrel-chested, dark-skinned men with steel strong legs thin as a deer's that carried them far and fast, thin, corded necks supporting narrow heads and hawk angry faces.

Chato had only twenty warriors with him here. Most of his Chiricahuas were on the San Carlos reservation while the restless chief and Cochise's son Nachite had been raiding below the Mexican border, bronco outlaws out for vengeance against all enemies, and everyone was an enemy.

The Mexican army had chased them, killed a third of those he had started with and driven the remnant north of the line. On the American side there was no relief. The troops were out and the Fourth Cavalry was scouring the broken land for the raiders.

Chato was driven, retreating under pressure to the only refuge he knew, the Superstitions. From time immemorial the tribe had looked on these brutal mountains as their final safe harbor. Following their habit they had ridden their ponies into the ground, then eaten them and gone on afoot. Their moccasins were thin and tattered, their bellies gaunt with hunger. A lesser leader would have taken his warriors back to the comparative security of the reservation. Not Chato, nicknamed Flat Nose since childhood when a pony had kicked his face, crushed the beak bridge back to the plane of his cheeks.

Routed, they had evaded the armies for more than three hundred miles, living on jackrabbit and snake, through the long arid stretches milking barrel cactus for the water stored by the thick, succulent plants. In other areas they knew of springs that kept them alive where most white men would die of thirst.

They had reached the craggy foothills three days before the treasure hunters, climbed into them and paused to rest, to dig pits and bake agave bread. As long as the plant grew in the southwest and there was time to prepare it the Apache would have that to fall back on when other food sources failed; they would have mescal to drink from its sap, bringing mystic dreams from the gods.

Here within the safe embrace of the mountains they could recover their strength, but they must not be careless. Chato set a sentry on a peak to watch the climbing trail. It was that lookout who spotted the dust of approaching riders on the flat land and flashed his signal with a polished metal mirror.

With the new rifle taken off a dead soldier after a skirmish Chato went up the peak. From there his eyes, keen as binoculars, studied the advancing party. It was not military. He counted eight riders, two extra horses and six burros with fat packs. Here were mounts. Ridden double they could carry all his men. Undoubtedly there was food in the packs.

He did not know what brought the travelers to the Superstitions but he suspected gold. The bright metal was an evil that had brought only death and defeat to his people. It had no value to the Apache. They stole what they wanted. There was no need for it. It was a curse that brought white men into Indian lands, men who were destroying the buffalo, the mainstay of their diet, were rapidly taking the whole country away from the tribes who had held it for generations.

But he welcomed the men below him. After horses and food Chato needed ammunition. There was very little left after the flight. Such a train as he looked down on would have an abundance.

He watched this full cornucopia make camp at the seep, dig a shallow water hole, build a small fire, cook and eat. Before full dark the men rolled in blankets for the night, very early for whites, suggesting that they were extremely tired.

Chato was tempted to hit the mat once, while there was some light, but he thought better of it. The light was going quickly and if they posted a guard, if there was an alert and a fight, one might escape. If that happened he could bring the Fourth Cavalry down on the band again. The chief had a wary respect for the yellowlegs. Indians won some skirmishes but in the long run the growing waves of soldiers rolled over them.

Caution told him to wait, let the intruders come deeper into the mountains, strike only when there was room behind them to hunt down any who got away. Caution also told him to keep a constant watch. White men were known sometimes to sleep only part of a night, then move on.

He sent the sentry down to the little bowl where the seep began in a trickle of water that flowed out of the rock wall, fell into a pool the size of a cooking pot, a stone worn hollow through ages of the drip, spilled over the lips and sunk into the coarse sand floor of the canyon. The Apaches were there and would send agave and a gourd of water to the lookout post. Chato would trust no one except himself to stay awake through the dark hours. The sentry also carried a warning that the band should stay ready to move if the travelers did.

With food and drink the chief settled himself in the cleft of a split stone block. Night came. Later the moon rose, slanting silver across the ragged crest, softening the harsh shapes of the slopes, easing the agony of the tortured land.

Nothing moved in the white men's camp as the hours passed. If they slept through until daylight, so be it. Chato kept alert. He had spent too many nights spying on Mexican and American cavalry, seeing them take a stealthy trail in the middle of darkness to let himself be lulled into carelessness here.

Around midnight with the moon overhead bright enough to make the camp clearly visible Chato was rewarded. A figure stirred, threw off his blanket and stood up. That in itself meant little. Many whites had to relieve themselves at night. But when a second man rose the Apache's interest quickened. Bodily function was not what they were about and there was a furtive care in their actions as though they wanted to avoid making the slightest noise.

The men slipped to the picket line, saddled two horses, lashed packs on two burros, led them up behind the guardian pillar, mounted and walked the animals up the canyon. The moon was plenty to see by, so the climbing, twisting trail presented few dangers.

Chato smiled. Two riders coming toward him were much easier to overcome than the whole column would be. He rose, worked a little stiffness out of his legs from their long crouch and ran lightly down to the bowl. By the time the two travelers reached the spring the ground had been swept of all sign that anyone had been there recently and the Indians were in the crags above where they could parallel the whites' advance and not be seen. Tempting as it was to drop down on the pair immediately Chato commanded no such move. If one were only wounded by a first arrow, and screamed, the peculiarities of the terrain could carry the sound on the breeze and warn the sleeping camp. The Indians could afford to bide their time until the new day came and the prey was beyond any possible escape.

Stringy, dour Eddie Brown and the chunky, heavy faced Bob Kenny had been with Avery Christian when they hit the stage that carried no passengers, only the treasure box that required two men to heft it when they had watched Wells Fargo load it into the coach.

Their getaway had been clean and as equal partners they were rich men. Until Avery had doublecrossed them, drugged them, made off with the box and all the animals, leaving them afoot, and they had neither seen nor heard of him in the year since.

It had seemed the hand of a kind fate when Burt Christian looked them up in their Tombstone headquarters, showed them Avery's letter and map and enlisted them to help recover what the letter said was fresh-mined ore. The drugging had taught them a lesson. They had profited by that twice now, once on the stage to Tucson when they exchanged the maps, and again last evening. They rode in high spirits through the night, picking their way over rocks and hard, sun-baked ground where they left no sign for anyone but an expert tracker, and none of the people they had abandoned, they thought, qualified in that ability.

A mile up the hill where it was safe to talk aloud Brown laughed, a rare sound from him, and said in his rasping voice, 'You want to make a bet on how long it will take our pals to figure out the old man's map is a ringer?'

'Huh-uh,' Kenny said with heavy humor. 'No way to find who'd win. We ain't going to see them again. What do you guess they'll do when it dawns on them the drawing they've got is no good?'

'Cry and go home. What else? There's too much territory up here to go poking around in blind. What I wonder is, why Avery waited a whole year to make a move and why he gulled his brother with that letter.'

'Smart. He knew Wells Fargo would be swarming over the country for months and he didn't dare come for the box until things cooled down. His brother is insurance that Avery isn't being quietly watched by somebody he hasn't spotted. Nobody would suspect Burt, he was in St Louis, so he could bring the gold out and Avery could grab it from him the same as he did from us.'

'Yeah. He's got a jolt coming soon. He must not know Burt would think of coming to us. But I'll tell you something, partner, I'm not drinking any more coffee until we dig up that box, split it, get out of these hills and lose each other.'

Bob Kenny's long jaw worked, he spat tobacco juice, his thin mouth looped up on one side. 'Same idea I had. There's plenty for the two of us, and that much gold can make anybody grabby. What do you mean to do with your share, blow it? I'm going to a big city, dress up and find me some rich suckers to invest in some projects with me, the kind they know how to make more dough out of.'

They climbed on in silence, wrapped in dreams. The eastern sky above the jagged crests paled. It would soon be day and the camp they had slipped out of would be waking. Down there the party would be thrown into confusion, scratching their heads. Or maybe somebody hadn't drunk enough of the dope to sleep through, had found the two gone, got the rest up and they were already in pursuit. The thought was strong enough to make Brown turn in his saddle, look down the switchbacks dropping behind and below.

He saw a brown, almost naked figure at the edge of the trail dodge behind a boulder and his breath sucked in, loud. Kenny glanced at him, then looked but saw nothing.

'What's the matter with you?'

'Indians down there. Let's clear out of this place.'

They spurred the horses, dragged at the burros' lead ropes, driving up the rocky canyon path. Chato was ready. The Apaches were above the whites, hidden in the tumble of the steep wall. The one Brown had seen had showed himself purposely, to strike fear, cause panic and flight into the ambush. He had succeeded.

Brown and Kenny made the top of the switchbacks and headed into a nearly straight stretch. There in the growing light the Indians rose out of the stones on the canyon's lip yelling a high, yipping cry. Kenny's horse bolted. He yanked it down, tried to turn it for a flight, collided with Brown's animal. The trail was too narrow there, with a long drop off the lower side, for the horses to pass the burros in the instant.

Both men flung off from the saddles for shelter behind the animals' big bodies. They had spent years in the Indian infested deserts and hills and knew first hand what small chance they had of escape here. Indians always wanted horses, wanted them alive. They would not kill these. There was safety in their flanks for the moment. Neither man was a coward and though they knew they looked at death they would sell their lives as dearly as they could.

Their rifles laid across the withers they looked for targets among the rocks and saw nothing now to shoot at. The Indians had vanished after their brief exposure. Kenny and Brown threw lead anyhow between kicking the burros, facing them downhill, hauling the horses around, backing down the trail, watching the rising wall. Neither looked to the side that fell away.

It was from there the real attack came. An Apache with a lance, another with a knife between his teeth, scrambled like silent shadows up the nearly sheer face. The flint tipped lance pierced Brown's thin back, came through his chest as he screamed. A dark hand circled Kenny's thick neck and cut the throat as deep as the spine. Kenny fell without sound. Brown heaved, rolled, kicked, then fell slack.

The Indians came out of the rocks like spiders. Four deployed below caught the frightened, running animals, hobbled both front and rear legs, then joined the group around the bodies.

Chato's second-in-command was already lifting hair with an expert twist of his knife practiced since his tenth year. Finished quickly, Ulzana presented Chato with Kenny's tuft as the chief's right and kept Brown's for himself. Nana and others were wrestling off the white men's coats and shirts, all that was wanted of the clothing. Trousers were an uncomfortable nuisance and no Indian foot, accustomed to the flexible, soft moccasin, would tolerate rigid boots. No-wa-zhe-ta, medicine man for the band, further mutilated the corpses to add powerful charms to his bag of ritual materials.

That completed the immediate tasks. Chato ordered the animals brought up and the party climbed the trail to a deer trace that took them over the rim to a wider, nearly level meadow of bare rock for a division of the other spoils. Brown's and Kenny's rifles went to Ulzana and Nana, since Chato already had one. The short guns were given to Nachite and a boy who had not yet earned a name.

The burros were unloaded, the packs opened. There were extra shirts which were kept, blankets which were not, jerked meat that was distributed to be sucked at right away, cold, hard biscuit impossible to eat until they were soaked. The Indians tried to chew them dry, gave up and tossed them aside. On the meat and agave brought with them and a water skin they made feast. Chato wanted to celebrate the boxes of ammunition for both rifles and short guns. Used with care it could supply them for weeks.

They spent the day where they were, dug fire pits, heated rocks in them, cut mescal, pounded the thick leaves to pulp and baked more agave, covering the dough with coarse sand as an oven. There was no hurry. The remaining whites would be a long while reaching the bodies Chato had deliberately left in the middle of the trail and when they did he was confident they would raise a racket he could hear across the quarter of a mile distance. He need not even post a sentry until the afternoon was half gone. He would let his tired broncos rest and take pleasure in their booty. When he did send a man to watch he came back immediately. The whites had already passed the bodies, had not made noise enough to alert the Indians and would soon be passing the deer trail.

Chato went to see. He looked down on six riders, four laden burros and two extra horses. The men would be armed at least as well as the first pair with good, far-reaching repeating rifles. His broncos had only the four guns taken from Kenny and Brown added to their lances and bows. All except he had thrown away their heavy guns when they had run out of ammunition. In an open attack even though there were many more Apaches than whites the fire power was too unequal. The chief would wait, ghost along beside the invaders, hope for another separation, watch for a chance to cut out one or another alone.

As they passed below him Chato studied the people at close range. Three strong young men with faces tanned by much time out of doors, turned up watching the rim, looking for Indians. But they would not see Chato and the sentry. There was a sandy-haired, light-skinned man and one older, thin and wiry as a bronco but also pale. Another, slight figure with long cornsilk colored hair in a thick braid that brushed the saddle. A woman. What kind of men would bring such a woman into the Superstitions for any reason?

The Apache wanted the woman. More, he wanted the horses, the pack animals for eating and for what they carried. Most he wanted the guns and ammunition. But to get them he would have to move with care and patience until there came a time to strike when he was sure of his game.

Chapter Five

The white camp at the bottom of the canyon held a conference. Burt Christian roused himself from his shock far enough to suggest that they stay where they were but out of sight, to wait until Avery's partners came back down with the gold. Ross Eaton told him that would not do. There were other ways out of the mountains and Kenny and Brown could be expected to use one of those, not backtrack where they could be waylaid. It was his idea to send Christian and his daughter back across the desert to wait in Tucson. He would take Smith and Jones and track the treacherous pair. What he did not say aloud was that in the changed circumstance he wanted the girl out of jeopardy if there was a fight when they found the others. He wanted his hands free to take on the highwaymen and the train robbers as opportunity offered. But Angela Christian would have none of that. If she did not trust her father she trusted Brown and Kenny less this morning and there was no way to be sure the rest of the escort would be more honest. Again the editor egged her on. Hannibal Heyes and Kid Curry exchanged surreptitious questions, puzzled at what Emile Chavez' real game was. The man was so bland, so easy going, enjoying himself like some conspirator whose plans were falling into place with the solid clunk of a safe being opened.

When Eaton surrendered because there was nothing else to do short of abandoning the entire project, when he mounted the truncated column and would have kept Angela in the lead with him, Heyes thought it was time to interfere, risk or no. The cop wasn't thinking, probably trying to juggle too many balls at once to keep a focus on anyone. He put his horse against Eaton's apparently accidentally and jarred him to one side.

Smiling an apology he said in a low tone, 'It's your say of course, but riding up on that pair could be dangerous for the lady. Shouldn't she lie back? The trail's all rock and we won't be moving fast enough to raise much dust.' He held his smile to minimize the criticism.

Eaton chewed his lip. It was indeed a lapse to see more potential harm from Heyes and Curry than from Brown and Kenny. But he would not let her spend the day alone with the train robbers. Externally they had too much charm and physical appeal for women. Their record held a long roll call of surprisingly intelligent and respectable women who staunchly defended them when questioned, had helped to make it impossible for the law to come up with them. But there was a compromise he could make and he put Angela in the care of Emile Chavez, back with the burros. The editor would maneuver her to advance his precious story, but that could not be avoided anyway.

Alone in the lead he took them up the steepening grade, concentrating on the ground, finding rocks recently scarred by iron hooves, stones kicked over so their damp under sides were turned upward; small but telling signs of what branches Brown and Kenny had taken where the canyon split as tributary arroyos came down into it from higher reaches.

He had not lost the way when, shortly after a noon rest halt, his horse shied suddenly, snorting in fright. Thinking a snake lay coiled in the trail Eaton drew his side gun, lifted his eyes off the rocks, hauled the animal down, a sharp grunt shocked out of him.

He raised his head higher for a quick scan of the rim and the rock tumble between, then jerked it to the rear. The burro directly behind him stopped at his horse's tail and the column halted. Burt Christian, half asleep in his saddle, his energy drained by his emotional turmoil, did not even open his eyes. Chavez and the girl were blocked below the tight turn of the top switchback. He could see them but they could not see the higher trail. Eaton schooled his voice, almost called Heyes and Curry by those names, cut the words short and tried again.

'Smith, Jones, come up front here.'

The tone was too flat, too empty. They lifted their rifles from the boots, ready to fire, had their own look up the wall while they kneed their animals past the train. Emile Chavez also studied the crest and as the boys rode by him they had their first good view of the sheltered eyes, bright, expectant, eager.

Coming abreast of Eaton, one on either side, they saw what had stopped him. Two half-naked white men mauled and left in grotesque death by human beings.

Eaton said, 'Brown and Kenny.'

Kid Curry swallowed hard. 'And Indians that aren't supposed to be around.'

Hannibal Heyes sighed. 'I'll go tell Chavez he was wrong and to hold the Christians down below.'

He put his horse downgrade again, picked up Burt Christian's reins and towed him back beyond the turn. A smile was hard to come by at the moment but he managed one of sorts.

'Be a little delay, ma'am, there's some obstruction to be cleared before we can get by it. You all climb down and take a break in the shade there for a while.'

Angela Christian was willing. This ride was harder than she had imagined, but she was confident it would be worthwhile. If they did not recover the gold that would be a blow, but on the other hand there were three men here who excited her as none of the tame city suitors ever had. She was much taken by Ross Eaton, big, strong, handsome, dominant, and she was feminine enough to find many signs that he was interested in her. But Smith and Jones were fun in a quiet way, their laughter easy at the evening campfires, about the only chances she had had to be near them this far. If there was a block in the trail above she thanked it for the extra time to rest and do a little dreaming.

Joshua Smith had dropped off his horse and she let him lift her down, feeling a tingle at his touch and the dark solemnity of his eyes. He brought down her blanket, shook it out and eased her onto it, then pulled her father off his animal, set him beside her, and still with closed eyes Burt Christian lay back and went to sleep. Heyes turned his back and cocked an eyebrow in a question to Emile Chavez who had not dismounted.

The editor had read Heyes' face and said softly, 'Digging takes a lot of wind when you're this high. I'll come along and spell you boys.'

Heyes saw no reason to stop him and he was curious about what the man's reaction would be to the proof of Indians in the area. He got on his horse and followed, coming abreast just as Chavez had his first sight of the bodies. Chavez reined in without haste. His mouth puckered to a tight O. He too took account of the surroundings as he tugged at his chin.

'Apaches, eh. Well well. This is interesting, isn't it? We may see a little action after all.' He peered through his lashes at Heyes. 'Scare you?'

Ross Eaton lashed out at him, tired of the puppet master poking and prodding. 'Quit it, Emile, this can be serious.'

Chavez did not ruffle. 'Certainly it can. Isn't that the spice of living? The edge of danger? There are four of us capable of putting up a show and the poor ragged-ass devils who did this didn't shoot, probably didn't have guns. This was hand to hand and well done.'

Eaton was sharp again. 'They have guns now, Brown's and Kenny's. A rifle and short gun each. Furthermore, they have coats and shirts and more than likely that map. Without it there's no telling where that treasure is. We're turning around now while we can possibly get out.'

For the first time Hannibal Heyes and Kid Curry agreed with a law man. They were already putting their horses about when Chavez spoke in a reasonable, patient voice.

'Let's not panic until we know the map is gone. Christian carried his in a money belt. We ought to see if these do. Joshua, do you mind a bit of gore on your hands?'

Joshua did. He did not want to touch the foul corpses, but with Eaton watching he could not refuse, show himself squeamish when the Wells Fargo man had already betrayed his own nerves. To his relief Kid Curry lifted a leg over his saddle, stepping down.

'I'll take one. Let's get it done.'

Heyes got down, drew his knife, walked to Brown's thin,

angular body calling across his shoulder, 'Eaton, Chavez, don't get hypnotized on this. Keep watch for company.'

Brown lay sprawled on his back. Heyes put a boot against the ribs, turned him over, bent and cut through the top of the trousers and belt, touching nothing, and with the knife point flipped the fabric wide. There was a canvas girdle around the waist. Curry stood waiting to see what it held. If the map was there Kenny need not be searched. Heyes sliced through the canvas, then had to take hold of one end to yank it from under the body. At least the blood on it was dry. Unbuttoning the pocket flaps he shook them empty of coins and bills, then had to dig into each for a paper that might not have fallen. There was no map. His lip twitched up for Curry.

'Your turn.'

Kid Curry found the drawing on Kenny. His job was cleaner than Heyes'. The chunky figure lay with the head downhill and the fluids from the slashed neck had not stained the trousers. He straightened above the body, unfolded the paper, read the lines and notes and fastened them in his mind. He would not forget the picture. Then he passed the paper to Heyes, who would not forget either. After that it would not matter if the map was lost again.

Ross Eaton and Emile Chavez studied it in turn, Eaton agreeing that it was a drawing of country he knew, that the landmarks matched places he had seen. He tucked it in his pocket.

'All right. Now I know where to go. But I don't know where the Apaches are. They can be miles away or they can be behind any rocks here waiting to hit us. We have to find out which before I take that girl one step farther.'

Heyes winked at Curry. So the cop was vulnerable to Angela Christian, and that information might be useful in some future delicate situation.

'I'll go scout around,' Heyes told Eaton, 'while you people clean this place up.'

The law man narrowed his eyes, showing his hostility for the first time. 'What do you know about Indians?'

'Enough. I've played tag with them before.' Heyes did not mention that in many a getaway from a train robbery he and

Curry had had to evade the tribesmen as well as blundering posses or expert manhunters. It had been part of the challenge that gave their old life its zest. Emile Chavez had spoken of danger as a spice and he wondered how a writer, an editor understood. The man was a riddle that he itched to solve.

Mounting, Heyes rode higher watching both sides of the trail. The downward slope was too steep for horses or burros, but somewhere the Apaches must have left the canyon track, and not too far away. They would be in a hurry to investigate their plunder. He found the deer trail where no attempt had been made to conceal the marks of the animals' scramble up the rocky trace. Leaving his horse ground-reined he climbed, stopped below the rocks that fenced the rim, put his hat on the muzzle of his rifle and lifted it slowly until the crown showed over the top.

Nothing happened. He edged higher, watched to the sides, saw no movement, but a downdraft washing over the slope brought him evidence that he was close, the smell of rancid grease used by Indians to groom their hair, keep the sun from sucking it dry and brittle.

Heyes crawled then, slow, particular that he did not dislodge a stone to rattle down and betray him. Lifting the top of his head into a cleft between two slabs fallen together to make a tent he could look down on the barren meadow.

They were there. One burro had been butchered, cut to ribbons and strips of meat hung roasting over a fire that gave off no smoke at all. He saw Apaches strutting in the white men's coats and shirts, finery that would soon bore them and be discarded. He counted twenty-one figures behaving not like a party on a raid but as if they were on holiday. Thinking about that Heyes decided he knew what they intended. If they had not yet discovered there were more than two whites in the mountains they soon would, then like wolves they would trail along looking to catch someone apart from the others where he could be picked off. Going for one at a time until only Angela Christian was left. Light-haired women were prized nearly as much as horses.

Satisfied, Hannibal Heyes crept down as carefully as he

had gone up, reached his horse and went back to where Kid Curry and Ross Eaton were piling mounds of head-sized rock behind a great slab that had slid from the rim and landed on edge with space behind it to contain the two bodies out of sight. Emile Chavez watched from his saddle, directing the work to small places that were not yet covered.

As Heyes paused at his side the editor bent toward him, eager. 'That didn't take long. Did you find sign of them?'

Heyes hid the sourness that was in his stomach and wanted to be in his voice. 'I found them. More than twenty. A quarter of a mile ahead, up behind the rim. Haven't spotted us yet, they're busy playing with their new toys. If we move now we may get past without their seeing us. Unless,' he faced Eaton who had straightened to listen, 'we chicken out.'

Ross Eaton's high cheekbone, stubborn-jawed face betrayed how sorely he was torn. With Brown and Kenny disposed of, with the map in his pocket and only Heyes and Curry to contend with he had a good chance to make a coup, net the outlaws and return Wells Fargo's lost fortune. Except for the Apaches. Except for a girl he was more and more convinced was unaware of her uncle's crimes.

Watching him, Kid Curry dropped Heyes a wink and told Eaton in heartfelt opinion, 'I'm for that, chickening out. Four to one odds and a yellow-haired woman to whet those broncos' appetite. It would take an awful lot of go . . . ore to be worth going loco for.'

Hannibal Heyes frowned at him, knew just what was in his partner's mind. It was hard to keep the Kid on target, staying out of trouble. He still thought of robbery first as a way of life, and now with the map to a treasure like a photograph in his head he wanted to turn back, lose the cop and the Christians, then return for the gold, just the two of them.

And they could do it. What must be in that green box would keep them living very well for years. Temptation tugged at Heyes. He had no scruples against taking from Wells Fargo. The growing octopus had ruined, was ruining too many small stage lines, banks, independent businesses, swallowing them whole to feed the expansion of its empire for him to have the least compassion for the express company.

It took a lot of will to look at the consequences. Ross Eaton too would go back, gather a band of agents like himself sufficient for fighting Apaches, and if the chest was gone from the hiding place he would think immediately of Hannibal Heyes and Jeb Kid Curry. They would be on the dodge again, hunted as they had never been hunted, and the pardon forever beyond reach. They would have to leave the United States and never come back. Heyes liked the country. He did not like Mexico nor South America and Spanish was the only foreign language he knew. An outlaw he did not mind being. An exile? No.

But again Emile Chavez was pulling his strings, saying airily, 'Ross, I've never known you to back down from a job. You volunteered to find the gold Avery Christian left up here. I couldn't admire you if you went back on your word.'

That tipped the scale. Hannibal Heyes looped a sardonic smile at Kid Curry when Ross Eaton pulled on his hat and squared himself.

'We'll go on,' he said, mounted, took out the map and rode down to the girl and her father.

Chapter Six

Angela Christian studied the map Eaton handed her, recognized it as the one she had seen in St Louis, remembered the landmarks that had escaped her, was especially beautiful to Eaton as she glowed with new excitement. He enjoyed that for a long moment before he told her what else had been found and what was in prospect.

'Kenny and Brown are dead, killed by Apache broncos. We found their bodies, butchered. Joshua Smith climbed the wall beyond here and saw a band of more than twenty. They have two rifles and two hand guns taken from the men and they have the two horses. But there are four of us who understand their ways and know how to fight them if we have to. If we are very quiet we may be able to slip by without their knowing it. If we are that lucky and the moon is clear we can travel until it sets, rest until daylight and ride again. We can be where the gold is in another two or three days. You and your father must never stray out of sight of all the rest of us. But if you would rather we will take you back to Tucson, I can get up a larger party and come back later.'

Burt Christian had waked, heard Eaton out and debated the alternatives with himself. Like his daughter, since Brown and Kenny's defection he had lost faith in everyone. If they turned back now he was certain neither would ever see an ounce of metal nor ever see these men again.

Before Angela could make her choice her father said determinedly, 'Of course we go on. With all due respect to you, Mr Eaton, too many people have looked at this map now and any of them could rush up here again. Smith and Jones, even Chavez could take the notion they'd rather have our ore themselves.'

'Not Chavez.' Eaton sounded dry. 'I've known him some years and wealth doesn't impress him, but I heartily concur about Smith and Jones and for all you know about me I might doublecross you too. Staying together is the best thing we can do. Angela?'

The girl had lost color when Eaton talked of the Indians, but now that the fortune was within reach again she would rely on this big, competent man's judgement that they could make the passage, the recovery, the return. The danger began to have a magnetic attraction. She had been in jeopardy before, in St Louis when a street gang had jumped on her and another big man had come to her rescue, beat them off, run them away. Fright had been sharp, quick, but as soon as he appeared she had felt an intense thrill as though she were wholly alive and aware for the first time. The same sensation grew in her here. Her smile came full and brilliant.

'Yes. I won't be afraid with all of you. You and Smith and

Jones, you're strong and clear headed. You'll do what you say you will.'

Kid Curry arrived then, bringing one of the blankets discarded by the Indians, torn in half, and tossed one part to Eaton, saying, 'Cut that in pieces and wrap the string's hoofs so the iron doesn't make noise on the rock. Jones and Chavez are working on the animals up there.'

Ross Eaton caught the fabric, turned his head to conceal the sudden narrowing of his eyes. The idea was shrewd, one he knew the partners must have used probably many times to slip out of pockets where pursuers had thought they had Heyes and Curry cornered. He despised the outlaws but he had to admit a growing respect for their abilities, and he had a wayward wish that they had used their talents on his side of the legal line. They would have made good law officers.

It took only minutes to muffle the hoofs, then the train got under way, Hannibal Heyes in front to signal where the Apaches were, Eaton shielding the girl on the inside of the trail, Chavez at her other elbow, Christian riding with the burros and Kid Curry bringing up the rear where he could watch behind.

From his lookout post Chato smiled at their effort to pass him silently, and let them go by unhindered. He wondered if the animals had worn these blanket moccasins all the way up the mountain or only after the bodies had warned the men. It did not matter. If he were killing the first pair again he would have hidden them and destroyed the signs of the attack so the rest of their party would not know his people were near, but that did not matter either. He would follow at his leisure, downwind where the Apache spoor would not be blown to them, approach close when they made an evening camp and be ready to knife any of them who went out of the woman's sight to relieve himself. In the morning he would follow again, watch for others to leave the group. He was in no hurry. They would not eat all their food nor use much ammunition in shooting game for fresh meat. He would need to make an open attack only if the loss of a member or members frightened them into flight, and they were now deep enough in his territory that none could get away.

But they did not stop that night for long. While there was still light they halted at a seep where animals had dug for water, deepened the hole, ate a cold meal rather than build a fire that would make odor the downdraft would carry through the canyon, unsaddled and unloaded to rest the animals, let them browse on the dry grass that followed the damp course of water beneath the stony floor. Angela Christian asked if the short, stiff clumps weren't too sparse to support much animal life and Eaton explained that there was more concentrated nourishment in this growth that had to struggle for survival than in that on well-watered flat land.

Heyes and Curry standing guard until full dark, when the venomous snake and spider population from the burrows where they hid through the heat of day and Indians wisely stayed in some place they had cleared, the party waited for the moon. The canteens had been filled, people and animals had drunk and napped and used the dark for nature's functions, when thc big bold disk that seemed within arm's reach rose over the sharp teeth of the mountain spine so quickly it looked like some hurrying live creature. They saddled, loaded and pressed on, Eaton again at the head, taking branches at the landmark places, remembering them from having chased another fugitive up these trails.

At the increasing altitude the night was cold, feeling colder after the withering heat they had been in so long. Kid Curry, seeing the girl shudder with the chill, unrolled her blanket and his and wrapped them around her, very pleased with the press of her fingers around his hand in gratitude. He rode close against one side of her, alone with her because the track was too narrow for more than two animals, the wall sheering up five hundred feet and dropping clean another five hundred to blackness even the moon did not dispel, the upslanting shelf turning sharp angles.

On the western faces where the cliff blocked the light the men dismounted, felt their way forward on foot leading the animals. Curry kept hold of the girl's rein, forcing her horse so close to the wall that she raised her leg around the horn and rode sidesaddle to keep from scraping her knee. Across the first stretch where nothing could be seen she closed her eyes in terror of the abyss so close on her other side, but from then on she kept them open, trusting in the invisible Thaddeus Jones to find a safe path. Trusting him, a fondness for him grew. Ross Eaton was bigger, stronger, but Jones' easy grace, his compulsive infectious laughter and gentleness toward her were having a telling effect on her. Terror gave way to a secret smile. She knew the impression she had made on him, it was in his expressive eyes every time he looked at her, but that was true of Ross Eaton and Joshua Smith as well. A whole life spent in St Louis could never produce such experiences as she was having in the Superstition mountains. Eerie, dangerous as they certainly were she found she loved them.

The moon sank before dawn while they were still on the perilous shelf. Eaton stopped them until the first gray light, then took them up a final mile. At the top other arms of mountain converged, created a wide bowl where ancient fast water that had created the deep canyons had brought down rock, churned it to sand, then to silt and built up a flat bed half a mile across. Grass grew thick there, nourished by the minerals released in the pulverizing action, irrigated with the confluence of streams now far below the surface but drawn up through the loose soil by a capillary attraction.

Ross Eaton rushed the party to the middle of the bowl. There they would be out of reach of the rifles the Apaches had if the Indians had seen them and were following, and he had small doubt they were. Little that moved in these mountains escaped their sharp, suspicious eyes for long. They made a camp, picketing the animals to graze on the stubby mat. They would eat and sleep through the day, the men taking turns two at a time to watch for dark figures crawling on their bellies from the canyons. The next night, Eaton said, would not be so rough, the trail climbed a mountain flank weatherworn to an easy slope.

Hannibal Heyes and Kid Curry saw the place as an ideal hideout for such hoot owls as they had been, and it was indeed the location Eaton's outlaw had run for, but the Wells Fargo agent had chased him on, higher into harsher country and caught him when he chose a dead-end box canyon that he could not climb out of.

Eaton now dictated the sentry duty. He and Heyes would stand one watch, Emile Chavez and Curry another. He would not rely on Christian, a city man, and he would not permit Heyes and Curry to stand together while he slept. It was too probable that knowing how the map read they would vanish like Brown and Kenny. But the editor and he could see that neither left.

Curry built a small, dry fire, heated the chilli and tortillas again, debated eating with Angela Christian but decided that was not politic with Ross Eaton on the scene and withdrew with plates for himself and Heyes. Straddling their saddles on the ground facing in opposite directions to watch both ways, the Kid frowned, uneasy.

'Where are they? My skin's crawling.'

'They're not crazy. Why should they show themselves? If they've seen us they know what firepower we have and probably can't match it. As long as we stay together they'll lie low until we start down. They'll take the risk then.'

'That sounds right.' Curry's eyes ranged over the edges of the bowl, back and forth, just in case, giving a low, rueful laugh. If it weren't there are so many of them I could be talked into ditching the cop and going for that box. Hannibal . . . ?'

'No. No and no. We've got months invested toward a clean slate and if we see this through we ought to earn extra points. Kid, when are you going to get that urge out of your blood. Do you want to have to jump the country for good?'

Curry said slowly, reluctantly, 'I guess not. But it seems a shame to be giving Wells Fargo such a hand.' Sharply, 'There . . . See him?'

The flicker of a brown movement among the rocks they had passed at the head of the gorge had been too fleeting. There was nothing to see when Heyes turned his head. Kid Curry crooked a finger at Ross Eaton and when the cop came over said he had had a glimpse of an Indian. The big man's face had showed increasing strain from the tension of uncertainty. Now it cleared.

'Good. It's a relief to know. I'll tell Emile and the Christians.'

Kid Curry pinched his chin. 'You'll spook the lady. Still, it's safer if she knows, and she hasn't panicked yet. That is one whole lot of woman.'

Eaton's mouth stretched wide and tight. He had not meant to give either of these outlaws any opening for a flare of temper, any excuse for Kid Curry's impressive draw, but the words snapped out like a reflex reaction.

'And not for you to think about. Just stick to your job.'

Curry blinked, shot a glance at Heyes, noted the quick frown of warning, half smiled and said mildly, 'Thinking is a private thing. Let's not get hostile until we're out of these hills.'

Eaton cooled off as if ice water had been thrown over him. He had made a mistake that could have cost him his life. He must not make another. These men were proving far smarter than any criminals he had met before. Unless they were provoked again they would not make their move until they and the gold were safely in the desert. It was there that he and Emile Chavez would have to take them prisoner. Or could he count on the editor for help? Would he perhaps stand aside and watch Eaton killed for the sake of a story? The thought of Chavez as that cold blooded had not occurred to him until this minute. In a flash he knew he must rule the writer out of his plans. He managed a strained half smile and went back to the fire.

Angela Christian wrung increasing admiration from all the men. She did not go to pieces when Eaton said the Indians were there. Cooly she scrubbed her tin plate with sand as she had seen them do, to conserve water, lay down with her head under her saddle to keep the hot sun off it, and went to sleep.

After dark they climbed again. As they turned up on the far side of the bowl Hannibal Heyes, watching the back trail, saw the fire they had left smoldering in a bare patch of sand where it could not spread, blaze up again and sent a low whistle along the train. The Apaches had moved in.

The mountain flank was dim under the stars but safe for

traveling. Before the moon rose a wind came up, cold and blowing coarse sand against their faces. They lifted their handkerchiefs over their mouths and noses, pulled their hat brims down to their eyebrows, kept their eyes on the ground except for quick checks ahead, but in those brief seconds the grit stung against their lids and slitted eyes, made them weep so tears ran down to soak the bandanas.

On the crest it became a howling gale. The animals constantly tried to turn tail to the blast until Ross Eaton gave up, called a halt on the bare rock slab of red sandstone, the unbroken strata that made a flat mesa top, and they crouched in blankets, backs to the wind. It lasted half the night. Thirst came and the canteens were very low. What water they had would have to last until they dropped into canyons again. But there were a few scattered barrel cactus, stunted, thick, looking like thumbs sticking out of crevices.

Kid Curry saw one close when the moon came, cut off the top below the spiny cluster, then cut off the ribbed rind of a section exposing the pith that stored moisture and sliced rounds of that to chew. It was spongy with a sticky sap, lightly sweet, and had saved many lives in arid land.

By dawn the wind front had blown through. They slapped off what sand they could, shook out the blankets, rolled them and headed downhill. It was not far to the X on the treasure map, Ross Eaton said. They could be there and gone before the Apaches could cross the mountain.

The downslope was soon split by a canyon head. Eaton led them into that and then a short cross draw in which a trickle of water ran on the surface, consulting the map now because this was new territory to him. Half a mile up the twisting draw they reached a spring. Instructions on the paper said the ore was buried at the spring. It was a surprising place, a flat, sandy floor between sheer cliffs a hundred feet apart. Against the foot of one wall was a rock font seven feet high and five feet across, a large cube of the red capstone, one of a long stretch of fallen rubble like it. Ten feet up the cliff a small hole let a jet of water under pressure from a higher source spout a foot horizontally before it poured into the basin beneath it and overflowed through a wide, worn groove. It looked like a man-made arrangement.

The first importance was to drink, fill canteens, water animals. When that was finished Ross Eaton read aloud from the map.

'*At* the spring. Where at the spring? What direction from it. He doesn't tell that.'

They studied the sheer walls, the rubble piles at the base, the sand floor. Kid Curry tried the floor with a pick and found a solid rock sheet only inches down. Nothing could be buried in that. Starting at the cube, working both ways from it, they began prying rubble away from the base, clearing it as deep as the floor it lay on. For ten feet in each direction they turned up nothing but red rock chunks from chips to blocks as big as the spring stone. It was hot, exhausting work with the sun rays shimmering up, reflected from the floor of the narrow cut.

Hannibal Heyes straightened, arched his spine back with a hand on his aching muscle, saying speculatively. 'At the spring. We are not *at* the spring. Jones, come down here and give me a boost.'

Kid Curry cocked an eye at his partner, understood and tucked in a corner of his lips. 'Last chance, Mr Smith. They're ready to quit and call it a wild goose chase.'

'Your brain's cooked. Come on.'

They walked to the cube. Curry made a saddle of his hands, Heyes put a foot in it and was lifted high enough to catch hold of the top and pull himself up. He had been there earlier, delegated to dip buckets of water and pass them down. It had not seemed odd at the time that the spring was only two feet deep with sand and rock below, but now he knew why. Pulling off his boots he stepped in, bent to throw the stones out, then dig his hands deep in the sand. Six inches lower his fingers felt over a flat surface banded with metal straps. The water was cold, welcome against his broiling skin. He found a square corner, moved his hand around that a foot, held his breath and lowered his head into the spring until he could reach a metal handle beneath the lip of a lid. Straightening, hauling up, he needed three tries until the heavy box tipped, sucking out of the sand under it. He left it there for a moment while he caught his breath, beckoning to Curry.

'Get up here, Jones. I need a hand.'

The faces lifted to Heyes had been doubtful. They changed instantly. Christian spread a snag-toothed grin. Angela's mouth opened happily. Ross Eaton's went empty. Emile Chavez' eyes, unsheltered, turned upward, lively and intent for a second, then they dropped and flicked from one person to the next until he had read the reaction of each. Kid Curry's mouth turned down on both sides. He motioned to Eaton to help him up the rock, got a knee on top, then both, looked down as Eaton moved away, spoke very low to Heyes.

'We can get back-shot up here, you know, now it's found.'

Heyes bent toward the handle and it put their heads close together. 'Not while there are hungry Apaches to get through. Later he'll make a try. Take hold and pull.'

Curry thrust his hand down and found a grip. 'Criminal, that's what this is.'

'It was, putting the box here. Now, heave.'

The chest came up slowly, heavy to begin with and clung to by the sand, but it did come. When it was on end, half above the water, they straightened to rest before tugging it on to the rock. Glancing down they saw Ross Eaton spread legged, his right hand spread on his hip just above his holster. If Kid Curry had worried about being shot so did Eaton, and he anchored his eyes on Curry's hand. Curry smiled down on him innocently and called to the girl.

'Here you are, ma'am. You want to catch it when we toss it?'

'Emile, Mr Christian,' Ross said without looking away from Curry. 'Go help bring it down.'

They went to stand below the partners. Heyes and Curry in one strong surge dragged on the handle, lifted, slid the chest up on the thick rock rim, balanced it there until hands reached up, then worked it over, tipped it, straining now to keep it from pulling out of their hold and falling on the men below. Only Chavez was tall enough to reach the hanging handle, waved Christian out of the way, chuckling.

'Swing it to the side and let go. It'll come down hard but it won't break.'

Heyes and Curry swung, let the box drop and Chavez could only guide it to land on its bottom. Kid Curry jumped beside it, backed away, watchful of Ross Eaton. Heyes pulled on his boots and followed, throwing a shower of water from his wet clothes. His attention was on the girl.

She was staring, frozen, reading the heavy stencil on the chest that read Wells Fargo, then she looked toward her father. 'Can that be Uncle Avery's? It wouldn't hold much ore.'

Heyes said quietly, 'Not ore. Gold. He mined it out of an Express company coach.'

'Stole it?' Her head snapped to Heyes, back to her father. 'He's a prospector, not a thief . . . Isn't he?'

Hannibal Heyes said softly, 'Open it, Thaddeus, let's see.'

Nobody really saw Curry's draw. The explosion bucked through the canyon, the sound racketing back and forth. The big rusted padlock flew apart and the hasp shattered. Curry took a step toward it but Heyes touched his arm to keep him back, nodding at Eaton. Ross Eaton was not going to be tricked into using his hands to lift the lid. Emile Chavez put a hand in Burt Christian's back and shoved lightly and the spidery figure dropped on his knees to claw at the lid. It did not give.

Curry said, 'Step back a piece and I'll blow the hinges.'

He did. Then Christian was kicking at the joint, finally taking a pick to it before the rusted seam broke and he could tug the top off. Hannibal Heyes spent the time whistling under his breath, his eyes on Emile Chavez, openly mocking. The editor answered with a merry smile.

Burt Christian squatted back on his haunches, gloating. The chest was filled to the brim with canvas sacks, full and bulging, patterned with small ridges like haphazard fish scales. He reached for the puckered neck of one, picked at the knot that held it closed and reverently spread the mouth, dug both hands in, brought them out filled with shining coins, exhibited them for a moment, then let them cascade back. No one spoke. Kid Curry's eyes were hungry on the chest.

Eaton's darted watchfully between him and Heyes. Angela Christian stared in horrified fascination at her father, realizing at last that he had known all along what they were looking for.

Then Emile Chavez' voice came, mild. 'Something else of interest is on the cliff top, gentlemen. A group of Apaches there appears curious about our actions.'

Chapter Seven

The bronco Apaches were indeed curious. So much so that Chato and his whole band had crept to the cliff edge and leaned out to see what the white eyes were doing at the bottom. The wall was a thousand feet high and not quite sheer, tilting out as it rose so that the Indians must expose their heads and half their torsos to have a view of the base.

Chato had made no move to attack so far because his curiosity was not idle. He wanted to learn why these people were in the Superstitions. He suspected they were hunting gold and wanted to be certain. If they had found it he must find where so that signs of digging could be obliterated, the gold hidden and the party prevented from getting out of the mountains. Word of a discovery reaching the white communities would launch an invasion of great numbers as it had in other Indian strongholds and there would no longer be security here.

Trailing these five had not been hard, and now the trailing was finished. Two had climbed into the spring and dragged up a heavy chest, shot it apart, and Chato's keen eyes could just make out bags such as he had seen the army transport its money in to the reservation. It was bad that someone had brought the box this far into his territory to hide it. He hoped it was the men below and not someone else who would bring a force back to recover it. And it was time now to think of getting rid of this group and taking the animals and provisions.

The broncos could not do that from the cliff top. The distance down was too great for arrows to carry true and the angle was treacherous for their three rifles. They had no ammunition to waste on uncertain targets. And now that the whites had seen the broncos they would be dangerous. It was proved as Chato dodged back out of sight, a gun fired and a bullet whined off the spot he had just left.

Hannibal Heyes said dryly, 'Missed him. What rattled you?'

Kid Curry shot the gun home to the holster, snapping, 'Eaton, get Angela behind the horses. They won't shoot near them.' Then aside to Heyes, 'Too much shimmer in the air. Looks like the rock's waving. You going to just stand out here?'

Ross Eaton had swung the girl to the far side of the closest horse, covered her body with his in case there were other Indians on the opposite rim from those they had seen and hustled her across the floor to the rubble there, shoved her into the shelter of a flat slab pitched against the wall and ducked in after her. Heyes and Curry snagged their rifles from their boots and dived under another stone. But Christian lagged, hating to move a step away from the green chest, but Emile Chavez caught his arm, spun him among the horses, pulled both their rifles, tossed Christian his and prodded him into the hole made by a flat stone lying across two others and crouched beside him. It was the first time Heyes and Curry had seen him do more than amble from one place to another.

Curry chuckled. 'He can scoot when he wants to.'

'Wonder what his hurry is. He's not going anyplace right away.'

There had been some draft through the narrow canyon but it did not move the air in their cul-de-sac. That was an oven. They watched the rim for an hour, seeing no movement, handkerchiefs tied over their foreheads to keep sweat from running into their eyes.

Heyes said at last, 'Are you as dry as I am, Kid? Cover me and I'll get us a drink.'

He left his long gun and while Curry studied the high rim sprinted for the horses, pulled canteens from the saddles, distributed them among the pinned down group, then crawled into shelter again. They rinsed their cottony mouths, swallowed sparingly, and continued waiting. The heat increased as the afternoon dragged on. Kid Curry groaned.

'A sweet stalemate this is. At least the broncos can breathe up there . . . If they're still up there. Maybe they're hunting a way down, and I wonder if this is a box canyon they can keep us blocked in. I could get bored with this place.'

'Oh, I don't know. It's cozy. Plenty of water, nice and warm, a string of burros if we run out of other victuals, interesting company.'

They talked to keep from going to sleep in the enervating heat. About the long-necked, long-tailed bird that appeared from a shading rock cluster and ran to another on the far side. Why does a road runner cross the road? To get on the other side. About the rattlesnakes that were surely in the deep recesses of the rubble waiting for night and a drop in temperature to come out in search of nocturnal rodents or a handy leg to strike. About their chances of getting out of the canyon alive with the Wells Fargo money.

Curry sounded disgusted. 'This job was a Jonah from the start. A cop, a pair of dim-wit road agents, an editor who likes to point people at trouble and watch them squirm, and now Apaches. We could have handled the rest of it, been on our way out, let Eaton have his loot, draw our pay and shake this country.'

'Forget the pay, Kid. If we do get the gold down these mountains we're going to have to pull a disappearing act before Ross Eaton decides he doesn't need us except in jail. We don't want to have to kill him, do we?'

As they watched both rims and up and down the canyon floor the sun set. Night came immediately to the bottom of the deep cut. Heyes and Curry crawled into the open, warning Burt Christian to come away from the rubble before the snakes began their hunting. It was still hot, the walls giving off the heat stored through the day, and it would be midnight before cooler, fresher air would bring relief. In the sudden dense darkness Ross Eaton's voice came.

'Smith, Jones, you and Christian keep your noses working so those broncos don't slip in on us. Emile, help me. Bring the pack animals to the chest. Water them and the horses while I load the sacks.'

Heyes smiled and touched Kid Curry's shoulder. Eaton did not trust them to handle the gold when he couldn't see them. Then let him and the editor do the heavy work. The water buckets were already filled and the animals picketed along the surface trickle where they could drink enough to keep them alive through the scorching hours just passed, but now they would need more to travel on.

The partners separated, Heyes walking up-canyon, Curry down, out of reach of the string's sweat stench and the sounds of saddling and loading. Christian stayed with his daughter. He wanted to handle the bags himself but he did not want to make Ross Eaton suspicious of his intention to steal them once they were safely out of Indian country.

Eaton packed the ammunition and a scant supply of food, leaving the bulk of it so the burros would not carry too much weight. If they got past the Indians they could live off the land until they reached Tucson.

In an hour they were under way. Starlight now gave a dim view to guide them and Eaton put Heyes and Curry in the lead where he could keep track of them, the girl and her father with Chavez midway of the train, and trailed at the rear. Emile Chavez played another card in his game of inviting peril for the characters of his story, suggested quietly that Heyes and Curry ride well in advance, risk ambush to give the girl the protection of early warning of attack, and the boys could think of no way to refuse.

It was a hairy retreat between the towering walls and worse when they reached the bottom and must turn into the wider, less abrupt hillside where the trail climbed again. The Apaches could be off the cliff and waiting there in the rock upthrusts where they could not be seen until they struck. But they were not. Carrying their rifles ready to use the boys walked their animals up the long grade, the roots of their hair crawling, spines tingling.

It was a very long night, as silent a ride as was possible, but at dawn they were at the high stretch of bare, flat rock and there had been no Indians, nor was there any sign of them when they crossed the meadow toward the narrow descending shelf. In the middle of the grass the boys pulled up until the train overtook them and Heyes asked Eaton, 'Do we lay over here again or push on? They haven't just gone away. They'll hit us somewhere. I think now it may come where they bushwhacked Brown and Kenny. I saw agave ovens in that bowl above the trail and they've probably gone there for bread.'

'We push on.' Eaton was definite. 'That shelf is too risky to go down in the dark and there won't be a moon until near morning. When we're within a mile or so of your bowl we'll rest and take the suspect stretch in daylight too. Chavez, don't give me any argument on this. Don't tell me Indians won't attack at night and we can slip past. That place is about as low on the mountain as they ever go and they want these animals and guns. They'll take chances to get at them.'

Hannibal Heyes had guessed right. Chato had not stayed on the cliff after he had seen the end of the white men's search. He carried a topographical map of the Superstitions in his mind, knew that the gorge was a short one and the cliffs pinched together a mile higher. It was as if a giant tomahawk had cleft the rock in the lower area. He knew too that only two trails down the mountains branched off from the way his prey had come up, so he took his broncos to the nearest of these and waited to see which way the white party went.

He had left Brown's and Kenny's horses and the live burro staked in the bowl because they could not be hidden in the rocks as he followed the whites on their way in. They had cleaned the long intestine of the butchered animal, filled it at the first water they came to, given it to the medicine man to carry wrapped around his neck and waist and taken what agave bread was baked. Now after the long trip to the cliff canyon the food was gone, the water drunk, and there was no more to be had until the branch of the second trail.

Thirsty and hungry the Indians kept vigil. The whites were long in coming. Chato smiled to himself. Sight of his warriors had frightened the men at the spring into hiding in that blistering cut for half a day. He knew they would only travel after dark and probably all the following day to get away from him, and fear made men make mistakes. His patience would be rewarded.

When Eaton finally passed the first alternate trail, going out as he had come in, Chato was relieved. The broncos could go ahead to the next turn and water, take a deer as it came to drink, using the silent arrow, eat and fill the intestine and watch in comfort. He hoped that somewhere one or more of the enemy would stray from the party and could be quietly killed. In any attack on the whole group against all their guns he was sure to lose men. He had already lost six on the flight out of Mexico, good raiders whom he regretted. But if they all stayed together he would have to fight them. His last opportunity if they passed the second branch would be at the bowl, for below that would be too close to the desert floor and there was much travel up and down the road, not unlikely army details looking for his fugitives. So he watched eagerly when the whites stopped on the ridge where the heads of two canyons topped together and the trails separated, willing them to come on by way of his bowl camp.

Ross Eaton had brought his party there by forced march. All the first night, the full day following and half the next night with only short rest pauses. They had then taken turns sleeping for six hours and with sunrise ridden another day. At the second branch he debated aloud.

Everyone knew the Apaches were stalking them. Heyes thought a confrontation would come where Brown and Kenny had been killed. They could take the other canyon but that way was two days longer down to the flat and there were more places for ambush on that descent. Emile Chavez voted for the new trail and the prolonged opportunity to study the tensions that ran below the surface, the frictions between the Wells Fargo agent and the train robbers and increasingly the surreptitious watchfulness of Burt Christian.

As a group they were held together by the need of numbers against the Apaches. They had to rely on one another. But it was a tight-strung, strained bond that was ordained to snap at some point. He himself, maintaining an outward calm to keep the fragile peace, was building an inner impatient expectancy of the coming explosion.

Hannibal Heyes saw him as an unknown quantity. In the crisis ahead would he stand aside, observing only, or would he take the part of the cop. It was safer, Heyes thought, to believe he would act. Up to a point he had been amused by the editor's machinations, but it was time to call a halt.

'If we're voting,' he said, 'I'll take the trail we know. Jones?'

'Uh-huh. And when it's good and dark. If we can't see much then, neither can the broncos. The only trouble is, arrows, lances, knives don't make powder flashes to aim at.'

Eaton and Christian also elected the shorter route and Chato smiled his satisfaction when the train moved out again. The Apaches slipped back like shadows, kept to the rocks away from the trail and went to their bowl, while the whites made a daylight ride.

Just before sunset Eaton stopped a mile above the deer trail into the bowl and since the Indians already knew they were in the vicinity Heyes built a fire, made coffee, heated the last of the beans and tortillas. They might as well finish what there was. It could be a last meal for all of them. The men smoked, tried to relax, to stay on alert balance for whatever was ahead, and almost succeeded.

Hannibal Heyes and Kid Curry knew from old experience that they would be at their most effective pitch when action came. Ross Eaton had the look of a man competent under fire. Burt Christian, a shrunken city spider, would be no help. Emile Chavez was a question mark. He wore a gun as though he were familiar with its uses and western newspapermen sometimes needed to defend themselves physically against those they attacked in print. Angela Christian was in the greatest hazard. Nothing in her St Louis experiences could have provided her the know-how to fight Apaches at night. Or in daylight.

When night came down with starlight barely to show the trail, they moved out. It felt better than doing nothing, waiting. A quarter mile above the deer trail the column stopped and the hooves were wrapped. The girl and her father were positioned between two burros each, on foot, leading their horses, and told to bend at the waist so that the little animals would shield them. If a gunfight came, Eaton wanted both of them where neither Indian weapons nor their own were apt to hit them. With lead flying the four white men would need as clear a field as possible to switch aim across.

In the rocks above the trail the single bronco Chato had left to keep track of the whites' advance saw how they disposed themselves with two riders in the lead, two walking among the burros, two riders at the rear. When they began moving again he ran down to Chato to alert him.

Chato was ready. He had used his time well, having boulders rolled from up the hillside to barricade the trail just above the deer trace, and there the broncos waited with strict instructions. No one was to use a gun, bow or lance for fear of injuring the animals that were so important. When the riders came the Indians were to jump on the horses behind the men and knife them silently, all except the yellow-haired woman who was to be captured alive.

Ross Eaton had a hard choice to make, whether to keep Heyes and Curry in front of him where they could not shoot him in the back or put them at the rear where Curry's fast gun could cover the rock wall as they passed. He took that chance because in the Indian attack his gun too would be needed. If they survived that he could look forward to their attempt to grab the gold and murder him on down the road.

Then nature intervened. A swift running bank of cloud spread over the sky, cutting off the starlight, leaving the canyon black. Eaton was pleased. They could pass unseen.

It did not go that well. At the barricade hidden in the dark his horse and Chavez' stopped, turned aside and stopped again. As his turned Eaton's boot scraped rock in the center of the trail. He spun, shouting the warning to head back uphill fast, thankful that the Indians he now smelled could see no better than he.

Chavez was already spurring between the burros, calling for the girl's hand and when she lifted it against his leg swung her up behind him, caught her rein, yelling at Christian to mount and ride, towing her horse in a driving run, giving the mounts their heads to find footing.

Ross Eaton stayed to empty his short gun into the rocks and heard Heyes and Curry also shooting, heard nothing from Burt Christian except his animal loping up the stony deer trace, guessed that an Apache had it and did not wait to find out.

Heyes and Curry heard two horses pounding toward them, a short gun blazing from the back of one. They flung themselves out of the saddles, hanging in one stirrup on the off-sides of their mounts where they were less apt to be shot, and when the rider had passed, the gun emptied and quiet, they chased after him, hearing Chavez' call come down that he had the girl with him.

The party came together again at the fire that still showed a bright red eye through the intense black, identified themselves by name. Burt Christian did not answer.

'Where is he?' Angela said sharply. 'Didn't he escape?'

'No.' Ross Eaton broke the news like swift surgery. 'I heard his horse go up the deer trail. He wouldn't take it that way.'

Hannibal Heyes said wryly, 'The pack train. Eaton, didn't you drive it up here? You left all the gold?'

The Wells Fargo man groaned. 'The surprise of the blockage . . . I forgot . . . There wasn't time to turn the burros and clear out of the ambush. We'll have to go back for it.'

'You go,' Kid Curry told him. 'It isn't ours and it isn't worth my scalp. We've got to keep going and pronto. Those Apaches had a taste of blood and they'll be baying after more. The only reason they aren't here now is that we have horses and they don't.'

'But my father,' Angela protested, 'we can't just leave him there.'

Emile Chavez told her gently, 'I am afraid we must, child. He won't know it.'

'Suppose he isn't dead, only wounded.'

'No Apache,' Heyes put in, 'ever left a white man only

wounded. Chavez, start her up the trail we came down and stay with her.'

The scudding clouds poured across the mountain, further blinding everyone. It was up to the animals to pick their way by scent. They climbed blind for two hours, then abruptly broke into the clear and light from a rising crescent moon. That made progress easier and they quickened the retreat, Ross Eaton making for the branch canyon.

The Wells Fargo agent was angry at the turn of events. He had been so close to succeeding in bringing out the stolen horde and bringing the train robbers to the justice they had well earned. Now he was back where he had started months ago. The Indians would bury the gold and there would be no map this time to show where it was. That would have to be crossed off. He would have to concentrate on Hannibal Heyes and Jed Kid Curry.

The narrow ledge made one of its frequent sharp bends. Once around that they could not be seen by pursuers, and Heyes, watching the rising wall called ahead to Eaton, pointing upward.

'Hold up a minute and look there.'

In some ancient time water had spilled off the crest, cascaded down, dug a channel that could be climbed for over a hundred feet to a small shelf littered with shattered stone.

'Jones and I can perch up there and pick the broncos off when they show, keep them back. You take our horses and keep going to that meadow. If you scare up any game, get it, and fill up on water.'

Ross Eaton's sour mood told in his voice. 'You want to tell me when to blow my nose too? We stay together.'

'He's right, Ross,' Emile Chavez said softly, laughing. 'Don't let frustration cloud your judgement. If Smith and Jones can cut down the number coming after us, even the odds some, we'll all have a better chance.'

Eaton grunted and watched with hot eyes as Heyes and Curry dropped out of the saddles, took canteens and rifles and climbed. Was he going to lose those men as well as the gold? While he sat with the girl and editor in the middle of a patch of grass the pair might be able to double back, skirt around the Apaches, make it back to the burro string and escape out of the mountains, cheat him of everything. Still, there were too many Indians for four men to take on at once.

He saw Heyes and Curry reach the ledge, climb over rubble and disappear, crouching down behind the natural breastwork, tossing jaunty waves. It was, Eaton had to admit, a place that could be held as long as their water lasted. He yanked his horse around harder than necessary, gathered the partners' reins and led off up the trail.

Chapter Eight

Much time passed. Because of the earlier cloud fog the horses had been slowed to a walk and should have given the Apaches on foot time nearly to catch up with the riders. Now, where were they? The moon was directly overhead, silvering the brutal heights, throwing crannies and ridges into harsh relief across the canyon but leaving the trail below Heyes and Curry dim and diffused.

Kid Curry stretched and whispered, 'Maybe they aren't coming. Maybe a horse and four burros satisfied them. I'd give a lot for a smoke.'

Heyes, watching the turn, clamped a warning hand on Curry's arm and leaned against his ear, his words a mere breath.

'They're here now.'

Curry snapped alert. One gliding shadow slipped around the canyon shoulder, hard to see except by concentrating on a certain point of rock and see it blocked out for a moment. Curry leveled his rifle, brought the muzzle down, judging the trajectory a bullet would take on the downward angle.

'Wait,' Heyes breathed. 'Let's get a covey in sight. I'll

work from the turn in, you hit the other end. Hold fire as long as your range is good.'

Curry nodded, tracking the dark figure in his sights. The bronco came confidently, passed below the ledge, went on, his head lifted, turning it, sniffing the downdraft for horse odor, then stopped and swung an arm to those behind. At once other figures flitted around the turn, running lightly, shadow silent.

Heyes counted in a whisper as they appeared in single file around the turn. Curry tracked the first bronco, figuring the distance that his rifle would carry. There were twelve in sight, strung out when the Kid spoke.

'Now.'

He fired, saw the Indian fling up his hands and pitch forward. Heyes took the one just showing at the bend. Calmly, mechanically, they worked from both ends toward the center just below. The broncos milled, not knowing where the withering volley was coming from, then panicked and tried to run back around the corner. None of them made it. No others appeared. It had taken seconds only, the time needed for each partner to fire six shots.

Neither spoke. They reloaded quickly on the offchance that the rest of the band had located their muzzle flashes, would scale the wall at a lower place and come on again above them. Heyes continued to watch the trail, Curry twisted to scan back and forth along the rim. In an hour they saw no movement anywhere.

Kid Curry stood up. 'I guess that's it for tonight. Cover me though. Up top.'

The Kid clambered over the breastwork and down the old watercourse, feeling his way, eyes on the bend the broncos had come around, using one hand to catch at rocks for balance, his rifle in the other trained on the turn. When he reached the trail he jogged to the bend, draped his hat on the gun barrel and edged it around, then when there was no reaction he eased along the wall until he could see the trail there. No one was on it.

When he reappeared he waved Heyes down but watched along the rim. Heyes slipped and slid to the bottom, walked to the bronco lying nearest the bend, made sure he was dead, and moved on to the others. Back at Curry's side they went on together, climbing from one body to the next, Heyes checking each while the Kid kept watch.

The first seven Heyes investigated wore knives in hide sheaths around their necks and bows or lances lay near them. The next two had carried Brown's and Kenny's short guns as well as knives, and small leather pouches hanging with the sheaths held ammunition. Hannibal Heyes gathered the guns and pouches and continued his search. The three at the head of the file had rifles. Heyes collected those and the bullets. Curry threw him a quick glance as they reached the last body.

'You look like a Mexican general with all that bristle. What do you make of these people?'

Heyes bent over the Apache who had led the dozen. It was a scrawny, half-starved figure with a copper colored face painted with vivid streaks of white and red, a bright striped woven headband with an eagle feather tied to it. The features were sharp, thin, the mouth cruel.

'Chief,' Heyes said. 'I'll watch while you have a look.'

Curry dropped his eyes as Heyes raised his.

'Ugly cuss. What about the others?'

'The other two with rifles would be lieutenant and medicine man. Pecking order. We got the leaders. I think with that kind of loss the rest have hi-tailed.'

'Hope so.' Curry relieved Heyes of half the arsenal. 'Let's do our own hi-tailing. Hannibal, how about this. You saw twenty-one Apaches when you climbed that deer trace down below and unless there were more you didn't spot over half are here. And I agree the rest have drifted off. What say you and I go for the gold and haul it out?'

'What I said before. No. Two reasons. Amnesty and pardon.'

'We could turn it in at a Wells Fargo office. There ought to be a reward.'

'Three reasons then. A girl with as much guts as looks up above with only two men to keep her alive. Suppose the broncos happen on them.'

'Oh.' Curry sounded startled. 'I'd forgotten about Angela. I was thinking of shaking the cop before I'll have to wing him.'

'Not at all like you, partner.' Heyes was dry. 'Start walking. Bring the hardware so Indians don't get hold of it again.'

They finished the climb to the meadow by daybreak, found Eaton and Chavez on guard and the girl asleep, took the men out of earshot of her and reported their success and surmise.

'If that's so,' Emile Chavez said, 'it should be safe to go down for the golden grail, speaking loosely. We can be there by afternoon.'

Tired as they all were, Ross Eaton insisted on going downhill at once. They woke Angela, got her on her horse and positioned her between Eaton and Chavez in front and the partners behind. Quickly but watchful they rode and saw no sign of Indians until the stretch where the dozen bodies lay. Eaton identified Chato.

'Flat nose. You can see why the name. I had a look at him once on San Carlos agency.' He recognized Ulzana and Nana and No-wa-zhe-ta the medicine man. 'Yes, the broncos have quit and gone to lick their wounds.'

Angela Christian shuddered and looked away from the carnage that the buzzards were feasting on, holding her kerchief over her nose against the stench that the heat was spreading.

They continued the descent and from above saw the barricade still across the trail. The burros and extra horses, the packs were gone. When they reached the ambush spot Burt Christian was also gone. The gold was gone.

Dismounting stiffly Kid Curry walked to the edge where the shelf dropped off, looked over and saw the body broken on the rocks where it had been thrown, signaled Chavez to keep the girl back, then stood enjoying Ross Eaton's fresh anger.

'Smart devils.' The words were a curse. 'They stayed here long enough to bury those bags and we'll never find out where. I give up. We might as well tear this rock heap down and go on before something else goes wrong.'

Angela Christian dismounted, sat down on a boulder at

the high side of the trail, rested an elbow on a knee and lowered her head into it, close to the end of her endurance and brought closer by loss of the father she had not trusted but had been her nearest kin and now by loss of the fortune that might have returned something to her for having recovered.

Hannibal Heyes idled toward the deer trace, studying the rock debris tumbled along the base of the shelf, then called back, sardonic.

'Over here, Eaton. We're not skunked yet.'

Ross Eaton trotted to Heyes, Chavez and Curry behind him. Heyes pointed at a pile of head size stones and rock chips no different from the other rubble except there was no sandy grit blown into the chinks or partly burying them. The Wells Fargo agent went to his knees, scrabbling the clutter away, and below the upper layer uncovered a section of canvas sack. Heyes winked at Curry, stepped back where the stones Eaton threw out of his way would not break a leg and raised his eyes for a look up the slope.

He was almost too late. An Apache had risen into sight, a bow in his hand pulled taut, and the arrow came winging. Heyes cried out and jumped and the obsidian tip whipped past his shoulder. A gun cracked near him. The Indian jarred back spinning, sprawled and did not move again. Kid Curry blew smoke out of the barrel of his short gun and kept it in his hand. Ross Eaton had snapped around on his knees, thinking he had been shot at and missed.

Hannibal Heyes said, 'Eaton, you and Chavez will have to pull those bags out and load them. Jones and I had better keep a watch.' He nodded up the hillside at the still, dark figure plastered against the red rock.

Eaton looked, then turned for a longer look at Heyes, at Curry, his temple throbbing. He drew and exhaled a long breath, brushed the back of a hand across his forehead, returned to unearthing the horde.

'Emile, take the saddle off two of the horses. We'll have to use them for packing and switch off riding. And start clearing a path.'

The editor glanced speculatively at the partners as if

doubting that both of them were required to see that no further Indians interfered, tucked a small mocking smile into a corner of his mouth and went to work. Surprising everyone, the blonde girl came to help him, throwing the lighter stones over the edge. Hannibal Heyes winced. Some of them at least would land on her father's body. He did not want her to see that.

'Angela,' he said, 'keep back from that drop off. It might give way and dump you down.'

Obediently she stayed in the center of the trail and lent her shoulder to the larger blocks when Chavez had trouble moving them alone. It took an hour to make a gap the animals could go through, for Ross Eaton to gather the heavy bags, tie a rope web to hang over the horses' backs and fasten the bags at the edges.

By sunset the party was ready to move. There had been no other Apaches but that was no guarantee they weren't around and everyone wanted to be out of the Superstitions as soon as possible.

It had taken half a day to come up this far on the trip in, but the packs each burro had carried were lighter weight than the gold two horses would be loaded with, and two men must walk. Hannibal Heyes, knowing from long experience how much the proceeds of a train or bank robbery slowed travel, estimated there was still a full twelve hours ahead before they were safely on the flat. It meant a long full night trek on top of the hours they had already spent awake.

They flipped a coin to choose which pair would walk first. Kid Curry lost the toss and Heyes elected to join him on foot, and since neither now trusted Eaton or Chavez to give enough attention to Apaches, Curry took the lead and Heyes the rear after an argument with Eaton. Emile Chavez had backed up the boys, claiming that he and Eaton ought to stay close to the girl to protect her and the partners were amused to see how uncomfortable the Wells Fargo man was, bracketed between them. It was plain in the set of his shoulders, the swiveling back and forth of his head that he thought the probability of their jumping him for the gold and Angela came nearer with every mile. For themselves they would not worry about the cop's expected move against them until he had the blonde out of the mountains and on the road to Tucson and had slept. By the time they made that road they would all be too exhausted for any sort of action before they rested.

They crowded through the gap and wound down the switchbacks to the canyon floor, and there changed places. Hannibal Heyes was delighted at Eaton's tension as he walked behind two notorious outlaws mounted, with two horses heavy with gold and the girl on another. His eyes never left them, never turned to the hills or the back trail.

Traveling throughout the night they alternated riding and walking every half hour and at daybreak passed through the great spires at the foot of the mountains, out of the Apache territory, went into the desert a mile and stopped. There they unloaded the animals, picketed them in the sparse dry grass, piled blankets over the tell-tale canvas bags and dropped on the hard ground, all of them dead to the world as soon as they stretched full length.

Chapter Nine

Hidden behind a stone column at the mouth of the canyon Avery Christian and two trusted Mexican village boys watched the descending party. Four men, none of them his brother, and his blonde niece. Five horses, no burro string, but two of the horses carried heavy loads. Two of the men walked with rifles in their hands, often looking back uphill, stumbling at nearly every step, weaving as though they were drunk or past the limit of their strength. Those riding sagged in the saddles, bowed, the heads nearly bumping on the horns, the men holding the girl from falling. Obviously it had been a hard trip and Apaches must have killed Burt.

But the survivors had the gold. That was the important thing. Losing Burt was not. He had taken the chance with his eyes open, well aware of what he was after. He was no innocent. At the time of the stage robbery Avery had sent him a copy of the *Tucson Sun* carrying the story of Wells Fargo losing a stage driver and fifty thousand dollars in American coin. A year later he had written the letter and sent the map, written about raw ore in case Angela opened the envelope, and since she was here she must have done that and been afraid if she did not come old Burt would blow with the whole treasure. Which he would have tried.

What neither of them had known was that Avery intended to waylay his brother if he succeeded in bringing down the fortune and take it away from him. Avery had not dared go for it himself because he suspected Wells Fargo's spies were watching anyone who went into the Superstitions through the early months after the hold-up, might even still be watching him. So he had holed up in Mexico to let time pass and interest fade. And there had been no one he could trust to send except Burt Christian.

The plan had worked. Soon he would be rich and safe among his new people.

He did not trail the party immediately, there was no need. Avery Christian knew where they would go, where they would stop, as done in as they were. In the rough brakes of Devil's Pueblo, off the trail where they would escape notice by other travelers. He would wait where he was, give them time to bed down, and with any luck he could come on them sleeping heavily and spirit the gold off without even a scrap. He gave them a long hour, then rode leisurely toward the maze of shallow arroyos.

When they found them the three dismounted silently and studied the drawn, haggard faces that winced and twitched in exhaustion. Avery Christian recognized Ross Eaton, the gambler who was whispered to be an express agent. He knew Emile Chavez by sight, but the other pair were strangers. One of his boys touched his arm and drew a forefinger across his own throat, eyebrows raised, indicating the sleepers.

Avery debated the idea of murder, decided someone might make a cry and wake others, and shook his head. He pointed at the pile of blankets and the rope webbing, indicating that the Mexicans should load the gold while he saddled the party's horses. They would bring good money as a bonus for the boys.

When the animals were ready Avery walked to the spot apart where his niece lay as if she were dead. He would put the men afoot, it was no skin off his nose if thirst drove them crazy and killed them, but the blonde was kin and besides she was too pretty a piece to leave here. On his knees he took the kerchief from around her neck, pulled his off, wadded hers, stuffed it into her open mouth and whipped his around her head, tying the gag. She did not wake, only groaned in her sleep. Neither did she wake when he threw her across his shoulder and carried her to the horses. Shrugging, he lifted her over the withers of his horse, mounted behind her where she lay back against him, and they rode out. None of the other people on the ground had moved. Now Avery was headed south toward Skeleton Canyon below Tombstone where they would cross into Mexico. Putting the men afoot would guarantee against pursuit. Walking, they could hardly be expected to cross that much desert.

It was noon before Ross Eaton stirred. He lay face up, his arms spread wide, the hat he had laid over his eyes blown off by a passing dust devil. The overhead sun beating on his lids woke him. He returned to groggy consciousness soaked with sweat, dreamed momentarily of a long cool bath and a shave, rolled on his side and rubbed at his burning eyes, opened them to blink away the burst of bright color spots that danced in them, facing the area where the horses had dropped, as weary as the people.

Through his blinking he saw they were not there. It could be that tired as everyone was they had not secured the animals, that they had got up and wandered off to better shade as the sun climbed. He sat up to look around for them and saw that not only they were missing. The saddles were gone. So was the gold.

Eaton swung toward Heyes and Curry, raging. Had the

pair stayed awake long enough to hide the bags? But why drive off the horses? Or had they moved them, ready for a getaway as soon as the worst edge of their tiredness was gone? He got to his feet quietly, walked a circle around where the animals had been, saw hoofprints in the grainy sand leading south and followed them a hundred yards.

Not until then did his weary brain register that there were many more prints than five animals would leave. They were not in single file but moving abreast. Eaton ran from one set to another and counted eight following the dry streambed.

To his shocked mind that meant Hannibal Heyes and Kid Curry had outsmarted him as far back as Tucson. They were not alone in this new theft. They had other gang members who must have plotted with them from the first and waited here in the breaks. He cursed himself for underestimating them. Instead of trying to do this whole job single-handed he should have wired San Francisco and asked James Hume, head of the express company's police, to send help he could rely on.

There was one thing he could finish and the time was ripe to do that, while Hannibal Heyes and Jeb Kid Curry still lay drugged with exhaustion and vulnerable. He could take them prisoner and salvage that at least.

Silently he returned to where they slept, knocked each lightly on the head to keep them out while he tied their hands behind their backs and took away their guns. Curry first, whose fast draw was the immediate menace, should he be one of those hoot-owl denizens who would wake from the dead the second his weapon was touched.

He used his own kerchief to bind one wrist, with the toe of his boot snapped him over on his face and fastened the other wrist against the first, pulled the side gun and tossed it away, tossed the rifle after it out of reach. The Kid remained limp. Grimly Ross Eaton swung to Heyes, tied him with Curry's kerchief and stood back, spread legged, eminently satisfied.

As he looked down on his handiwork Kid Curry groaned, moved his shoulders, found that his arms could not respond. His eyes flew wide as he struggled to sit up and he sat gaping at the law man above him, then spun his head toward Heyes and shouted.

The shout roused his partner and Emilé Chavez. Heyes came up thrashing, clumsy with his arms pulled to his back and a kerchief run under his belt, tied in hard knots to hold them there, his head throbbing. A short glance showed him Curry's like predicament. In the noon heat he did not waste energy fighting the bond. He sat quiet, warily eyeing the cop.

Emile Chavez got to his feet slowly, came to stand near, take in the trussed outlaws, then looked quizzically at Ross Eaton.

'Why here? Why now?'

Eaton's expression was like a hungry wolf's, his tone flat. 'Look around. Hannibal Heyes and Kid Curry here, finally nailed down. But they pulled a fast one. They had some help that picked up the gold and our animals and vamoosed south. Three more riders working with them.'

Both boys rolled to their knees, their feet and made a full turn to see the whole area, too stunned to protest at once. It was Kid Curry who first thought of the blonde girl. In a single spring to the top of a boulder for a better view he located the spot where he had last seen her. She was not there, not even her blanket. He shouted again.

'Angela. Angela Christian. Where are you?'

There was no answer. Ross Eaton's breath sucked in through his teeth, loud. He ran. In the loose grit of the blown sand footprints were plain. Her small boots going to the place. Larger boots beside them. The larger boots returning, angling toward where the horses had been, deeper now, a man carrying some hundred pounds.

'They got her,' Eaton yelled. 'Kidnapped her.' Hands balled into fists at his sides he stalked back to confront the partners, flushed and eyes blazing. 'What kind of men are you, damn you.'

He aimed a fist at Kid Curry's face and swung from knee level. The blow staggered the Kid. He stumbled and crashed down, his lip bleeding. Before Eaton could throw another at Heyes, Emile Chavez caught his shirt, pulled him off balance and dumped him sprawling on his back. Chavez dropped astraddle of his chest, pinning him.

'Whoa up, Ross. Think a minute. Why would these boys . . . ?'

Eaton fought to rise but Chavez was stronger than he looked and kept him down. Supported on his elbows Eaton bellowed.

'For a hostage. Get off me. They're Heyes and Curry and wanted from hell to breakfast.'

While Kid Curry sat up, rubbing his jaw, Hannibal Heyes found his voice, conciliatory. 'And you're Wells Fargo, Eaton. It's nice to have that in the open. But we didn't have any part of this. We didn't take Angela, we didn't take the gold, we haven't had a gang for months. Somebody else is taking a hand.'

'Don't try to con me.' The words were an oath. 'You're in this up to your scalp.'

Heyes shook his head vigorously. 'No way. No.'

'With Avery Christian. Yes.'

Curry gaped, swallowing. 'We are? We never saw the man.'

'Who else knew anything about that chest, where to find it?'

Chavez said smoothly, 'I vote for Avery, but not for these boys. Ross, it looks to me as if Christian intended to double-cross his own brother and he brought two men to help. He'll have to split with them and two more would cut the pie more ways than if he'd shared with only Burt and Angela. Why? Look at it another way. Heyes and Curry are too professional to let that gold out of their sight in the care of a man who would cheat his family.'

While Heyes and Curry stood on tenterhooks, Ross Eaton's face showed his mind begin to function, to back away from certainty of the partners' guilt.

Kid Curry breathed, barely aloud, 'Avery or whoever, they've got some hours start and are mounted. We can't catch up on foot and Angela's in trouble.'

Emile Chavez arched an eyebrow. 'Maybe not. Avery's her uncle and gold has its charms. She may have gone willingly. The loveliest rose has a thorny stem. But we're unlikely to learn unless we find horses soon.'

Eaton dropped back, his lips stretched tight against his teeth. He lay for a moment, then lunged up, tossing Chavez aside in his surprise move.

'Horses at Phoenix. A six-hour hike. And a telegraph. And,' he shot a baleful triumphant look at Heyes, at Curry, 'a jail. On your feet and move out.'

Curry got up, sounding hopeful. 'Our guns? That's good hardware and expensive. We take them?'

'You won't need them where you're going.'

'They can be sold, give us tobacco money.'

'Too heavy on a walk.'

Again Emile Chavez interceded. 'Ross, you could take the ammunition, let them carry them empty.'

Eaton regarded him hotly, then shrugged. 'If they want to tote that weight, I guess . . . '

He walked to Curry, stripped the cartridges out of his belt, felt over him to be sure he did not have more, relieved Hayes of his, then shoved him roughly against the Kid. Opening Heyes' trousers belt he looped it through Curry's and fastened it again. They could walk side by side but could not try to take off in opposite directions. Last he dropped the short guns into their holsters and slung the rifles around their necks.

They walked through the hot afternoon. Eaton found cactus to chew for moisture and ripe prickly pear. Peeled, the red fruit had a sugar content that would sustain energy if it supplied little real nourishment. They rested briefly every few miles and went on, Hannibal Heyes and Kid Curry ahead like Siamese twins, Ross Eaton behind, a gun in his hand, Chavez beside him. Eaton carried the weapon because he did not trust the editor. In his zeal for his story Eaton would not put it past the mischief-maker to try to release the prisoners for the joy of watching the fireworks.

It was a miserable day for the partners, uncomfortable enough to balance over the broken, tumbled ground with their hands tied behind them and held together at the waist so their hips constantly rubbed against each other and every step brought the long guns banging against the legs and knees.

Chapter Ten

During the rest stops Hannibal Heyes used all his considerable persuasiveness to convince Ross Eaton that the cop still needed him and Kid Curry to locate the girl and the gold. During their years, he argued, they had learned all there was to know about how outlaws thought, the sorts of trails they used to escape detection, the kinds of places where they holed up, the by-ways into Mexico, toward which he was sure Avery Christian was headed. As earnestly as he knew how he urged that Angela Christian had won their unwavering admiration, that it was most important to both him and Curry to find her safe, whether or not she was involved in the robbery.

To no avail. The Wells Fargo man plainly was torn, deeply interested in Angela Christian, but that was a personal matter. Duty must come first and first duty was to see this pair of outrageous outlaws locked away from society. After that, he said, he would spread a net of law to hunt down whoever had the gold. And the girl.

Footsore, utterly weary, utterly disgusted, Hannibal Heyes and Kid Curry were marched into Phoenix long after dark. Hours before they had quit talking. It was a waste of breath they needed to survive the long hike across the blistering desert.

The only people in the town still awake were concentrated in the two saloons. The wall lamp in the sheriff's burned, the outer door stood open, but there was no one there. Ross

Eaton prodded his prisoners inside. The grille of the single cell swung wide, the cubicle was empty. The key on a large brass ring hung beside the desk. Eaton lifted it, put his hands on the partners' shoulders and shoved them through the grille hard enough that they stumbled across to the bare bunk and fell on it in a tangle. Both would have preferred staying there on the straw mattress. Eaton would not let them. He locked the grille on them, then called them back to the bars to untie Heyes' hands and left him to take off the rest of the bonds. He hung the key on its hook, beckoned to Chavez and took him toward the saloons hunting the sheriff.

Separated, the partners sagged on the bunk and massaged their stiff arms. Kid Curry was glum.

'Pigheaded cop. They're all alike. No imagination.'

'If they had imagination they wouldn't be law men. It's a dull life and the pay isn't all that good.'

'Ironic, isn't it. We break our backs trying to go straight. We play his game straight, pass up fifty thousand when we could have had it a dozen times, and what's the thanks? The amnesty blows up in our faces.'

Heyes said thoughtfully, 'Chavez. With his quirks we might arrange a scoop for him, tell him if he'll get in touch with Lom Trevors he can have a big story first when we break it.'

Curry's voice was hollow. 'If we ever see him again. As far as he's concerned we're caught and he'll lose interest in us. He'll go sniffing after Eaton or go home and write what he's got.'

'Probably go home. I doubt Eaton can catch Avery Christian north of the border and if he gets as far as the Sierra it could take years to track him down. Chavez knows him, knows it will be a wild goose chase from here on. Let's get some sleep and tomorrow's a new day. We might be able to talk this sheriff into contacting Lom. Porterville might demand custody and when Lom understands he just might let us jump.'

'Spoil his reputation by letting us escape? Fat chance. Good night.'

Kid Curry lay back on the bunk, taking the wall side so Heyes could share. It was crowded but softer than the floor, than the rocky sand of the last many days and nights.

Ross Eaton and Emile Chavez found Al Norton, sheriff of Phoenix, in the second saloon and pulled him out of a poker game. Eaton showed his identification and tried not to boast when he said he had locked Hannibal Heyes and Jeb Kid Curry in Norton's cell and gave a brief of the capture.

'I can't swear they had a hand in this last grab but it doesn't matter. They've got a record so long they can be shut up for a hundred years. I'll leave them here for a while but they're slippery customers, don't let go of them.'

The sheriff took quick affront. 'Mister, I never lost a prisoner yet.'

'Don't start now. I've got to wire Tucson and Tombstone. I don't know where the rest of the gang is headed but I think into Mexico and I want them cut off before they can cross the line.'

To mollify Norton, Eaton bought a drink at the bar, then left for the telegraph office. Chavez lingered and the Phoenix sheriff grumbled.

'Wouldn't you know it would be tonight. For the first time in two weeks I didn't have anybody in the cell. Now I get these two dumped on me to spoil the evening and I'll lay you odds Eaton won't even cut me into the reward. Well, nobody made me take this job. I'd better have a look at these prizes.'

Norton flapped through the louvered doors. Chavez sipped a second drink, then he too left the saloon, whistling under his breath.

Ross Eaton had snapped the padlock on the sheriff's office and Norton fumbled in the dark for his key, let himself through the door and walked to the grille to look at the notorious captives. Both were sound asleep, one on the bunk face up, spreadeagled, the other in the same position on the floor where Curry had unconsciously forced Heyes. Al Norton studied them, muttering. Instead of the brutalized masks of hardened criminals that looked out from the posters he had seen of them the expressions these two boys wore held the innocence of children, untroubled, even vulnerable. Suspended as they were in deep sleep they both appeared totally helpless.

The sheriff studied them for a long moment, trying to tell whether they were playing possum, faking, but the eyes, sunk so deep in the sockets that they might be gouged out and blind, indicated exhaustion. Neither would give any trouble this night. The grille was securely locked, the key hanging twelve feet away on the far side of the desk where it could not even be seen, much less reached by any trickery, and the poker game Ross Eaton had pulled him out of was a good one, the cards falling hot to him. Norton flicked a finger off his hat brim and returned to the saloon.

Down the dark, empty street Emile Chavez watched the oblong of light play out of the glass top half of Norton's door. He saw it elongate when the panel was opened, saw the tall bulk of the sheriff come out, turn to close and lock the office and walk rapidly away.

When he swung through the batwings two blocks along Chavez went briskly forward, picked the padlock without trouble, lifted the cell key off the hook when he was inside, went on to the grille, called the boys' names. He got no response and rang the big key along the bars the width of the cell, then back. The rattling noise brought action. The partners clawed to consciousness, sat up, stared.

Hannibal Heyes yawned so widely his jaw nearly came unhinged. 'Can't you let a man rest, ever? You come here to gloat?'

The editor dangled the key in a pendulum swing, smiling sleepily. 'If I let you out what would you do first?'

'Ride after that girl.' There was no hesitancy in Kid Curry.

'I thought so. That's where the story is and I want to get it. We can ride together while Ross waits for answers to his wires and rounds up a posse.'

'Ride what? We haven't got horses and we're broke.'

Chavez fitted the key in the lock but did not turn it. 'Your word you won't run out on me?'

'Have we so far?' Heyes was unusually short. 'We won't. Besides Angela we've got a big stake in bringing that gold back to Wells Fargo. Believe that.'

Chavez smiled mildly. 'A good editor always believes what he's told until he learns different.' He turned the key, swung the grille wide. 'I've got horses up the street.'

Hannibal Heyes and Kid Curry took one short second to look wide-eyed at each other, then pressed into the office past the editor. Chavez closed and locked the grille, hung the key in its place, opened desk drawers until he found boxed ammunition for rifles and short guns, filled his pockets. Heyes and Curry had jumped for their rifles that Eaton had stacked against Norton's gun case. At Chavez' motion they waited until he stepped to the street, raked his eyes both ways along it, and beckoned. Then they peeled out, swinging against the wall where the light did not touch them, waiting again. Chavez closed and locked the outer door and led them at a trot up the dusty street where the sidewalk would not echo their steps.

Three horses waited ready for travel. Saddles, blankets, promising looking grub sacks, canteens. Heyes and Curry ran their hands over two animals. They were heavy chested and felt sound. The three swung aboard and walked the mounts out of Phoenix to keep harness noise to a minimum, then spurred east.

Ross Eaton missed the escape. He fidgeted in the telegraph office waiting for messages, chewing his nails, and when they came, assuring him that both Tucson and Tombstone would block the border crossings, he looked for Al Norton at his office. The door was locked and the lamp showed him no one at the desk. Swearing in disapproval at such a *laissez-faire* way of running a sheriff's business he headed for the saloon, found the man at the poker table and once more took him out of his game.

Norton looked at the swollen, red rimmed eyes. 'Man, you ought to be in bed. Did you get your answers?'

'I haven't been in a bed for two weeks and there's no time for one now.' Eaton was tart. 'I want those thieves before they hit Mexico and lose themselves in the Sierra del Norte. I'd never dig them out of there. You get up a posse to go with me as soon as possible.'

Al Norton had little relish for the idea. Still, Wells Fargo was immensely powerful and it could be worth while to cultivate this agent, so he tried to sound enthusiastic, calling above the noise in the room.

'I want five men to ride right away. Meet me at the livery.' In a lower tone he told Eaton, 'My saddle's at the office. We'll stop there on the way.'

Ross Eaton set a fast pace down the sidewalk, impatient at the time it took the sheriff to unlock his door, and crowded in close behind him. While Norton gathered his rifle from the case, loaded and crossed toward the saddle in the corner, Eaton indulged himself with a look into the cell.

It was empty. Too small and well enough lighted that no one could hide even under the bunk. Hannibal Heyes and Kid Curry just were not there. The Wells Fargo agent yelled and rattled the locked grille. Al Norton jumped a foot, staring at the man who pivoted around the desk, slapped at the key hanging there, shouting.

'They're gone. How did they get out?'

The Phoenix sheriff swung to look and said stupidly, 'They couldn't.'

'Then where the hell are they?'

Norton stood before the cell. 'They didn't fly.' He shoved his worn hat back with a thumb, patted the outer door key in his pocket, felt his face burn bright. 'Somebody picked the lock and let them out.' He stalked toward the door. 'The livery . . . see if they got horses or are still in town.'

They stormed to the barn. It was dark and the posse was not yet there. Ross Eaton cursed.

'Where's the night man?'

Norton panted. 'Old Sours owns it, he's too tight to hire one.'

'Where is he? Get him fast.'

The sheriff sprinted into the dark and was back in five minutes trailing a squat man buttoning trousers over a night shirt. Eaton yelled at him as he turned in the runway.

'Any horses missing?'

The square jaw thrust out belligerently. The man stopped to light a lantern, then ran on to the corral at the rear, was gone briefly, then reappeared, bellowing.

'Three gone.' He ducked into the tack room, calling from there. 'Three saddles, blankets, bridles, packs.' Turning the air blue he carried the lantern on to the office, Eaton on his heels and Norton behind.

In the middle of the scarred, cluttered desk ten twenty-dollar gold pieces were stacked on a paper bearing a single word written in a hand as precise as copper plate. *Thanks.*

'Well.' Sours grinned. 'More than the whole shebang was worth. Good honest fellows.'

Eaton shuddered, looking at the delicate hand. 'Chavez. Damn him.'

'Who?' Norton watched Sours dribble the coins through his stubby fingers.

'Edits the *Tucson Sun.* Thinks he's God. Turning Heyes and Curry loose, that's going too far.'

'How do you know it was him?'

Ross Eaton slammed a fist against the word as though that would obliterate it. 'I know his writing.'

Norton was bewildered. 'But why would he let those train robbers go?'

'Because he's crazy. And crazy enough to go with them. All he cares about is a story. He's gone baying after my gold and my girl. I'll scalp him.'

Ross Eaton pulled himself up short, astonished at what emotion had slipped out under his stress. Then he pushed the words away. The posse was there, laughing, excited at the prospect of a chase, whoever they were after, as a break in the monotony of days that ran together, all alike. Eaton rented another horse and gear, the sheriff saddled his black and the party took out at a gallop, filling the runway with rising dust.

In his impatience to be after Heyes and Curry, Ross Eaton gave no thought to provisions for the trail that might prove long. It was a disgruntled, disdainful Sheriff Norton who hauled down the rush for an hour to wake the general store keeper and commandeer supplies, while the Wells Fargo agent belatedly thought to send additional wires announcing the outlaws' escape.

Chapter Eleven

Hannibal Heyes, Kid Curry and Emile Chavez drove for Devil's Pueblo and the trail of the stolen animals. The walk to Phoenix had seemed endless but the fresh horses covered the ground in a fraction of the time. It was only midnight when they reached the brakes and a sliver of a sickle moon gave barely enough light to pick out high and low terrain. They found the right arroyo, did not go down into it but followed it north a quarter mile, then descended and made a dark camp.

If when Ross Eaton discovered the loss of his prisoners he came charging this way tonight he would not find them. Emile Chavez had had not even the short sleep Heyes and Curry had enjoyed in the jail and they could not follow tracks without light. Empty as their stomachs were they would use the night for rest, eat when they could see what Chavez had brought, then go after the thieves.

With first light and five hours solid sleep they made a cold breakfast on water, bread and meat Chavez had raided a hotel kitchen for, again leaving payment. Not knowing where Ross Eaton was, a fire was dangerous.

Refreshed and fed they picked a silent way along the rim of the arroyo, studying the bottom ahead, making no bend past which they could not see until Curry had surveyed beyond it on foot. He returned from a sortie near where they had lost Angela Christian, gold and horses, making motions for quiet, pointing a half circle to warn Heyes and Chavez to detour. They made a wide sweep and came back to the dry course well below and beyond other twists in the rugged cut. There the Kid laughed.

'The cop's there all right, with the sheriff and a posse of five. Looks like Eaton gave out. He's dead to the world. The rest are squatted around a fire with coffee and grub. Let's put some space between us and them.'

Returning to the rim they followed it until a small rock-slide let them down to the bottom without leaving sign, easily found the prints of the earlier passage and spurred in their wake until their animals needed a stop. There the partners thought they were far enough ahead of Eaton's posse to make a coffee fire. Hot as the day was a scalding drink laced and cooled with whiskey the editor had thought to bring was welcome, revitalizing. Riding with the relaxed Tucson man and free of the stern, intense Wells Fargo agent was a reminder of the old easy days. Kid Curry looked on him with affection, lifted his cup in a toast.

'This is more like. A hot trail to follow and welcome aboard the Sierra de la Madera del Norte Express.'

'A hot trail?' A corner of Chavez' mouth twitched in amusement. 'How many hours are those sharpies ahead of us? Sometime today they'll cut the Phoenix to Tucson road and that will be churned a foot deep with tracks heading both ways. How do you decide which ones we want?'

Kid Curry got up from his crouch and beckoned with a crooked forefinger, conspiratorial in the way he bent and stalked from the fire to the wide path of hoof prints, squatted beside one and drew a rut around it.

'Barred shoe.' He smiled up at the standing editor. 'You know, when a horse has a weak hoof the blacksmith forges a strap across the open end of the shoe to keep the horn from spreading. Somebody's riding an animal like that and if we're really lucky it will break down along the way. Anyhow, it's easy to trail.'

Back at the fire Hannibal Heyes had another thought. 'They'll cut the Tucson road, yes, but will they take it? Seems to me that's a long way around to Mexico. In their place I'd think about a shortcut, but I don't know this part of the border too well. Chavez, is there a reason they shouldn't drive straight south?'

The *Sun* editor pursed his mouth, looking off to a map in his head, and was slow in answering, slow in his words.

'They could. Lot of dry stretches between water holes but

it could be done. There'd be say three days across a prehistoric lake-bed, baked and cracked like a mosaic, then they'd hit the Gila. Plenty of water, shallow. Cross that into mesa country and another dry jump to the Santa Cruz. Bear west across to Santa Rosa Wash, dry except in flash floods but there's a subsurface stream. Follow that to its rise, then there's a twenty-five mile haul over the Quijotoa hills to the border. Lots of country with nobody in it. Maybe.'

Heyes arched a brow. 'Why maybe?'

Emile Chavez had a sleepy, crooked smile. 'In Phoenix Ross Eaton wired Tucson and Tombstone and elsewhere to throw a net along the line. There's likely to be company all through there.'

'Tombstone?' It was a yelp from Kid Curry. 'Why Tombstone? That's way east.'

'True, but there's water clear to Mexico, down the San Pedro, by-passing Tombstone ten miles west of town. That's the trail I'd take. Avery Christian, if it's him, doesn't know about Eaton's wires.'

Hannibal Heyes thought back to the days when he had led the Hole-in-the-Wall gang on many a chase that evaded a posse, and pontificated with mock solemnity.

'The quickest way to butt square into trouble is most often the shortest distance between two points. I don't know how smart Avery Christian is but he's got a pretty shrewd track record so far in planning ahead. Chavez, I'll go along with you and let's get about it. Ross Eaton isn't going to sleep forever, he'll be breathing down our necks if we stay here much longer, and while the gold is going to slow down the animals carrying it they're still a good day and a half ahead of us. Shall we ride?'

The barred horseshoe led them south to the Gila river and there turned east along the north shore. There had been no indication that Ross Eaton's posse was closing the gap behind them. This was empty country, no land in which to run a horse to death, and Wells Fargo's stolen horde was not so important to Sheriff Al Norton that he would take risks. Hannibal Heyes and Kid Curry knew the breed well, had played tag with them for years. He and his deputies would ride as far as the Mexican border but if they had not overtaken the thieves by then he would not cross. Eaton would cross, alone. Boundary lines meant nothing to the express company police.

At the river the dead ashes of a fire showed where the men they followed had camped. Heyes and Curry rekindled it just before sunset when the red flames would not make a beacon the posse could see from any distance. Emile Chavez unwound a fish line from his hat band, baited the hook with a cube of salt meat and caught a ten-pound catfish for a fresh supper. They unsaddled, the partners thought for the night, but over the food and coffee Chavez proposed a different plan.

'The Gila runs east, then turns south and becomes the San Pedro. That's the way our people will go, close to water. You're gamblers, we could make up a day on them if we go on tonight, angle across and down, cut the San Pedro below, if you don't object to a dry, night ride.'

'Sounds good,' Heyes agreed. 'Give the animals an hour or so to rest and graze, take ourselves a swim and we'll be as good as new.'

The river was warm, sluggish, and lying in it the gentle flow soaked the grime out of their bodies. Hannibal Heyes could feel his pores opening, sand washing out of them, his skin absorbing moisture to replace what the days of sun had drawn out. They dressed without drying, replenished the canteens, saddled and swam the horses across as dark came.

Chavez set a course by the stars, south-southeast, the base of a triangle those ahead were going around. By dawn they reached the San Pedro, swam that to the east side and there again saw the barred shoe that proved the editor's guess was correct.

Now they were far enough ahead that Eaton was no longer a concern and were a good deal closer to the kidnapped girl, if she had been kidnapped, and to the gold. According to long habit Heyes and Curry left the trail, camped in the thick strip of cottonwood and tule where the animals could be hidden and there was forage for them. They ate and slept until noon.

The land began to lift into broken, brush-covered hills. Three days later they entered the pass called Texas Canyon, east of Tucson, and pulled off into a side draw. Curry had a campfire laid to cook the rabbit Heyes had shot in the afternoon. The Kid was ready to light it when harness jangled and hooves drummed down the main cut below. Heyes sprinted up through the black lava tumble, looked over the top of one and saw the riders. A paunchy man wearing a star led them. Heyes counted twenty others as they swept by without a glance toward the draw. They too were headed south toward Tombstone, but it was doubtful that they could locate the gold thieves north of Mexico and they had ridden within a stone's throw past the outlaws Ross Eaton was so anxious to recapture.

Heyes returned to Curry and Chavez saying, 'Patrol. Let's eat and move on. We'd better ride nights from here to the border and check that hoof in the mornings so we know we're still trailing it. There's no telling how many posses and bounty hunters are on the prowl for us.'

Emile Chavez took over as cook that evening. He dismembered and boned the jackrabbit, a tough, stringy animal that would be all but impossible to chew if roasted, cut it into small pieces and boiled it in the coffee pot with a sprig of sage. In an hour it was edible, the broth tasty, a filling meal with the tortillas the editor baked on a hot flat stone.

Then they left the short canyon and paralleled the stream. The night was bright with stars, busy with nocturnal hunters that fell silent as they passed, and they heard nothing of other humans. Riding until dawn they located the barred shoe still leading south, drew off into a thicket-choked coulee and spent the day. Kid Curry heard a rustling in the brush, investigated and found an armadillo sluggishly foraging. When he moved toward it it curled into a ball within its horny armor and lay perfectly still. Because a gun shot could draw visitors he clubbed it with his rifle butt and they dined on its delicacy that night before taking the trail again.

Morning came and brought a surprise. The barred shoe print was not there, nor were those of the other horses. The men and the girl had not come this way. There had been no rain to wash out tracks.

'Great,' Heyes said. 'Where did we lose them, Chavez?'

The editor tipped his hat forward, looking chagrined. 'I thought they'd stay clear of towns but they must have turned off to Tombstone and we missed it in the dark.'

'Now what do we do?' Curry was disgusted. 'Backtrack in daylight? The country's probably crawling with fortune hunters I'd as soon not run into.'

'Nobody's looking for me,' Chavez offered. 'I can cut across and see if they went through there. It shouldn't be more than ten miles. I'll be back before dark. You hole up around here.'

Hannibal Heyes lifted a warning finger. 'If Ross Eaton is pushing the way I suspect he may beat you to town, spot you and trail you back here. Watch yourself when you ride in.'

'What else? I'll make a hoot owl yet.'

'Let's find out how soon. Where do you mean to ask questions? The saloons? The livery?'

'No.' Chavez' lips twisted, mocking. 'The *Tombstone Epitaph* has a rear door and Johnny Clum has a nose for news even itchier than mine. Where are you going to be?'

'Around.' Heyes was laconic. 'We'll keep an eye out for you.'

The editor laughed at the patent mistrust in the tone and rode off toward the east. The partners watched him out of sight, then took their horses up the rocky hillside where they would leave no marks.

Kid Curry said edgily, 'It makes me nervous, him going in there alone. How do we know what he'll tell this Clum? We might be smart to head straight for Mexico, then swing east to the road down from Tombstone and see if we can pick up that shoe again there.'

'Now? And run smack into a crowd panting after the money on our heads? I'd rather sit tight until we find out whether Chavez thinks he'd have a better story plus a fat reward for turning us up. Wait until afternoon and we'll move in closer than he'll expect us to be.'

Chapter Twelve

Angela Christian's uncle Avery, her father's half-brother, had been the prince charming of her girlhood dreams in St Louis. His actress mother had bestowed on him her good looks, her flair and charm, and Angela was always dazzled by his occasional visits to the drab boarding house her mother ran to feed and shelter her daughter.

Her father had been a will o' the wisp, appearing and disappearing without notice, making no pretense of supporting her and her mother. Distrust of him had been instilled in early childhood when he would 'borrow' money from his wife and never return it.

Avery was different and always welcome. When he turned up with no more notice than her father he brought gifts, jewelry and bonnets for the mother, silver souvenir spoons from places he had been and pretty dresses for his niece, and he played the gallant to them both.

She had not seen him in three years, but when his letter had come it had been so in keeping with her memories of him that she had not in the least doubted he had found a rich mine and was giving the ore to her and her father. It was added proof of his generosity.

It had been a shock when a Wells Fargo green chest was dragged out of the spring, filled with bright minted coins, another when the escort Joshua Smith suggested Avery had mined it out of a stagecoach, that it was stolen, and no one had said otherwise. But there was so much shocking on that trip that this new picture of her uncle had not made much impression.

When they were out of the Superstitions, exhaustion and letdown had overwhelmed her in a sleep so deep she had only woken from it in the morning, coming to consciousness slowly, on a horse, thinking she had been riding so many days and nights that this was part of a dream. But it was not. Then she became aware of an arm around her holding her against a strong body. It was unreal. She straightened and looked around. Into her uncle's laughing face. She gasped and choked on the gag in her mouth.

Avery at once took it out, saying sympathetically, 'Poor little Angela was so tired she didn't even know when we rescued her. Now you're awake we'll stop and have some breakfast.'

She smiled uncertainly, remembering his teasing, wondering how he had found her and what he meant by a rescue, too confused to ask questions. He stepped out of the saddle, lifted her down and held her arm until she found her balance. She turned to look around her and saw two men in conical hats with round, mahogany-colored faces and large white teeth showing behind wide grins. They too got down, only a little taller than she, dark eyes bold on her, talking rapidly in voices that ran up and down in quick cadence, a language she not know.

She also saw that besides the horses they rode they led a string of others, three saddled, two heavily loaded, and recognized those as the animals her party had brought out of the Superstitions. She watched the dark men immediately take the packs off and knew from the way their arms strained that the gold was in them. More and more bewildered she turned again to Avery with the beginning of fear.

'You kidnapped me, didn't you? What did you do to the men I was with?'

His laugh was free and full. 'Left them sleeping like babies. I had to take the horses so they wouldn't catch us. Don't worry about them, they only have a thirty mile walk to Phoenix. I left their water and guns. Your Wells Fargo friend will see they make town safe and sound.'

Angela Christian sank to the ground, her knees weak and trembling, ready to cry. 'Uncle Avery, I don't understand. Why did you do this?'

He crouched beside her, his eyes dancing as she remembered when he had a joke to tell. 'For a fortune, honey, that Wells Fargo owes me from way back. They're the worst kind of robber barons, a ruthless crowd who ruin anyone they consider in their way. Me for example. I had a little freight line going some years ago, beginning to make money, a good legal business. They burned my wagons, burned the goods in them, stole my teams. Now I'm burning their fingers. That's the way of the world out here, Angela. It's raw and hard, a man has to be strong to survive.'

'But stealing their gold, that's not honest . . . Who did you mean, my Wells Fargo friend?'

'Ross Eaton. Didn't he tell you when the "ore" turned out to be money? No, he wouldn't, he'd think you knew all about that chest and try to fool you until he could get you to a jail and arrest you.'

'Oh no.' The words were shocked. 'He's a good, courageous man. And he likes me. I could tell, the way he acted.'

He lifted a lock of her long, pale hair, tugged it lightly, traced a finger down her face, smiling. 'I am sure he did. I'm sure the others are head over heels in love with you. We don't see girls who look like you do now here on the frontier. But his kind, dedicated agents, are afraid of their emotions, they'll cut their hearts out in the name of doing their duty. As I said, I rescued you. If I hadn't you'd have found yourself in prison for years.'

She was silent, the sense of unreality spreading, giving her the feeling that she had slept through some strange transformation, had woken to a world totally different from the one she had thought she understood. Here was her uncle, as handsome as she had ever seen him, carrying gold he had admittedly stolen from the express company and claiming it as his right. She could see no guilt in his manner. And she could not make his description of Ross Eaton fit the big, competent man with whom she had felt safe even when the Apaches had attacked. Would he really have arrested her for going after what she had innocently believed was a gift from Avery. Then there was her father's death, his murder. This man smiling at her had sent the map that had led Burt Christian into the mountains when he must have known the danger, yet this morning he had not so much as mentioned his half brother. She looked at him more closely.

'Uncle Avery, I don't know you at all, do I? Do you know what happened to my father?'

He sobered, lifted and dropped his wide shoulders and his voice went flat. 'I can guess. But he knew what he was doing. And why. And he was thoroughly selfish. Remember what he did to your mother's life. After her death he'd have done the same to yours, hung himself around your neck to take care of until he got restless and ran out again. I'm not really sorry he's gone. Now there are just the two of us left and we have money enough to last all our lives in Mexico. Forget what's past and look ahead, accept reality, honey. Come with me and I'll teach you how to take the best of living.'

She had known precious little of that. The only bright spots for her had been his visits. There was a lustiness about him, an aura of adventure that radiated from him like a fresh, exhilarating wind.

She thought of Ross Eaton again, of the editor Emile Chavez who seemed to take life as a game much different from the dull monotony she had known. And Smith and Jones who showed an exciting zest for everything they did. All of them had proved themselves able at surmounting the many hazards of the mountains, and with them she had felt for the first time that she was wholly alive. If that was what Avery Christian meant by the best of living she wanted to continue it, and suddenly she believed he had a right to the gold, a repayment for the business they had robbed him of. Laughter came.

'Yes, I'll go with you. Where?'

He was plainly pleased. 'To a little village high in the Sierra del Norte, the great Mexican mountains. Tony and Pedro there come from it, it's called Janos.'

She looked to the dark pair. The round, flat faces, black, hard eyes and thick-lipped mouths looked as cruel as the Apaches had, making her draw back.

'They're friends? You trust them?'

'With our lives. I saved theirs when a firing squad was

about to execute them for a bandit general they were fighting. Come meet them.'

She rose, uncertain but curious, and followed him, noting again the grace of his movements, as if he floated rather than walked. They had finished unsaddling and built a fire, set out food, and stepped back as the Christians approached, pulling off the tall pointed hats and holding them against their own shirts, incongruously shy. Avery introduced them as the Rojas cousins. They acknowledged her in strongly accented English, bowing to both the girl and her uncle, squirming to please as if he were their idol.

They cooked, served, and built her a brush shelter under a cottonwood, spread a blanket in it for her, then lay down on the far side of the tree with Avery to sleep through the morning.

In the afternoon they continued south to a river and camped beside it. They did not hurry, often switching the heavy load of gold to different horses as they swung east along the Gila, then south again following the San Pedro. Two days later they entered a landscape such as Angela had never seen, skirting a dry lake so vast they could not see the other side, a flat, blinding white expanse. They by-passed a town and stopped in broken country at midday.

There Tony took a spare horse and rode off. Twenty-four hours later he was back, leading the animal that now wore pack saddles bulging with a new food stock and miscellaneous supplies in sacks tied across its back.

They spent the night where they were and took up the ride in the morning. That day they paused on the rim of a sharp drop looking into a narrow, barren gorge where nothing grew, a desolate, brutal looking waste. It appeared to the girl that the floor was littered with white, fallen branches, yet there were no trees. But when they descended the treacherous trail to the bottom and passed the first cluster of what she thought were sticks she saw it was a human skeleton, dismembered by animals and bleached lighter than ivory. Others were a mix of human and animal bones.

Angela looked off at the hundred or so similar grisly remains in horror. 'Uncle Avery, what is this? A battlefield? Why weren't they buried?'

Christian shrugged. 'Nobody cared. I told you this is hard country. Some years ago a Mexican smuggler gang got together a treasure of gold bars and what we call 'dobe dollars, Mexican coins with a higher silver content than the U.S. uses. Supposedly ninety thousand dollars worth. They loaded it on a mule train and tried to bring it north. Damn, trusting fools. One of them was a spy for Curly Bill Brocius' Arizona sharpies and he like to broke his neck crossing the border to alert Bill what was coming. He couldn't locate Bill but he collected some friends and waylaid the train here. This is one of the roughest parts of the Peloncilla mountains. All they had to do was sit up top where we were and shoot down at the Mexicans. Some of the smugglers got away, abandoned the mules and those scattered until they were chased down and shot, and the Tucson Ring turned a nice profit. Place has been called Skeleton Canyon since then.' He turned a crooked smile on his niece. 'It's said to be haunted. Do ghosts trouble you?'

She knew he was teasing but she could not restrain a shiver and an uncertain tone. 'They never have, but neither did Indians until I saw them. I can believe anything of places like this.'

'We'll be out of it tomorrow. See the mountains on the horizon?' Avery indicated a distant ridge of red stone peaks. 'Those are in Mexico, the Chiracahuas. We'll take the Skeleton through the hills east, then San Luis Pass south.'

Further into the bleak valley they stopped at a surprising spot where a clear spring reflected the sky's deep blue, a waterhole, Avery said, that never failed, even in the driest season. The canyon was a long hot climb to intersect the descending San Luis trail, and when that bottomed out in rough, rocky country the Rojas cousins sent up a triumphant shouting. They had been silent and tense until then. Now they had crossed into old Mexico and felt safe from pursuing posses.

They laughed and swaggered until they neared Agua Prieta, then turned sober and watchful again, though they entered the town openly. There were men on the streets, Mexicans and Americans, who waved welcome that Avery returned. Some wore loose white shirts and baggy white trousers and woven leather huaraches on their feet. Others were in some sort of uniform, carrying carbines, bandoliers, crossed over their chests.

Smiling at all, throwing salutes as though they were close friends, Avery told Angela in a low tone, 'Keep close to me and don't talk to anyone. Some of these are bandits who'd cut our throats if they knew what we're carrying. Others are Rurales, the Mexican force that corresponds to the Texas Rangers. There's a garrison here, so we must move carefully. You and I will drop off here at the cantina while the boys take the string to the livery for a rest.'

Angela Christian looked along the sorry streets. Like Tucson the town was fairly large, built of mud, the structures flat roofed and so low she thought her uncle and those of his height must bend over to pass through the serape hung doorways. Filth and flies abounded in the dusty roads where no sidewalks lifted boots to a more solid surface. Fifty thousand dollars would be a king's wealth in such a place. In a small mountain village it could certainly be a lodestone for cutthroat thieves.

Again she had a flash of doubt about Avery Christian and living with him under such sordid conditions. Any house she would find clean and comfortable must draw suspicion that it held more money than the entire population would see in their lives. The Wells Fargo fortune, whether or not he had a right to take it, appeared now like a millstone around their necks, a constant danger to their lives. Suddenly she wanted to be rid of it.

She wished Ross Eaton had it back. He must be hunting them, partly she hoped because of her but surely for the gold. But would he cross the national boundary? A sense of being abandoned in a foreign land she knew nothing about, not even the language, brought a fear she had not felt in the Superstitions with Eaton, Smith, Jones and Chavez and she longed for the safety of their company. But she was her uncle's prisoner, kind and gay as he was. She saw no way of escape, of returning the stolen horde to the north.

Avery was out of the saddle, lifting his arms to swing her down. Tony and Pedro led the animals past them at a pace suggesting they were all asleep. Angela's uncle took her elbow, turned her unhurriedly toward the low door they had stopped before, held back the bright blanket and ushered her through.

The room beyond was dark after the sun-dazzling street. They waited at the entrance, Avery skinning off his hat, the top of his head brushing the crooked pole rafters. A single lamp with a smoked chimney hung from the center pole and as her eyes adjusted, its glow showed her a cramped space, a saloon counter, hand hewn tables and chairs where men ate and drank tequila, mescal, home-made beer that stank like parched corn. Other smells were strong, cooking beans and chillis, stewing goat meat.

Angela heard female voices in running chatter but the women were out of sight behind another striped curtain at the rear, apparently in a kitchen area. She saw only one, at a table with two dark, mustachioed men with black, lank hair stringing over their shoulders. The woman was young, full blown, an olive-skinned beauty, raven hair in a pyramid of coils and held there by a tall tortoise-shell comb. A sateen red blouse and sequined, voluminous purple skirt marked her as hostess.

The customer's gabble of talk that Angela had heard from outside cut off abruptly as she came in. The tableau was silent, frozen for the moment it took her to see, then the hostess spun up from her chair, a short girl on her feet, and with a small pleased cry of surprise ran to throw herself into Avery Christian's arms as he stepped from behind Angela. He laughed and kissed her with gusto, then held her away, chuckling fondly.

The girl fought his hands, pressed against him again, went on tiptoe to whisper at his ear, a question, Angela thought as she overheard the rising tone. Avery bent his head again to hers, whispered, 'Si. Oro. Oro,' and covered the exchange of words with another extended kiss.

The gold was the girl's first concern. She immediately had

another. The delighted face turned stormy, the dark eyes sparked and she jerked her head angrily toward Angela, said in fair but sharp English, 'What is this you bring here in my face?'

Avery Christian teased her with silence for a moment, then turned her to face Angela squarely, laughing, speaking low.

'My niece from the States. Without her I would come empty handed. Angela, this is Dolores, Tony's sister. She'll be going with us.'

Dolores' antagonism was like a blow. 'You never told about a niece. I don't believe you. Send her out.'

Christian took her small chin in one hand, pinching his nose against hers as he held her eyes, his smile wider. 'You think I'm crazy, pet? Bring a woman in here who isn't a blood relative? She's my brother's daughter. Ask the boys when they come from the livery. Burt was killed and I'm all she has.'

Gradually the dark girl cooled down, slapped Avery's hand away and said doubtfully to Angela, 'Maybe yes. This man, who can trust him? He charms like the serpent, then . . .' She slashed a long finger across her throat.

Christian slapped her buttock playfully. 'You'd better trust me if you expect to go with us. Now rustle us up some decent food, I've had a belly full of trail grub.'

Dolores tossed a shoulder and went toward the kitchen, her firm hips swiveling, came back with a tray of pottery mugs and napkins to a corner table and shooed away the two men at the one next to it, leaving it isolated enough for private talk if voices were kept down. She poured beer for Angela, tequila for Avery and herself and as they sat down an older woman came with a pot of hot boiled kid, then brought another of beans cooked with red chillis and a basket of steaming tortillas.

Avery made approving sounds, rolled a tortilla into a cone, scooped goat from the bowl, handed that to Angela and rolled another, scooping beans for himself. There were no dishes and the corn cone was hot to hold, the meat near scalding. Angela shifted it from hand to hand, nibbling as soon as she could bear the food in her mouth and was pleasantly surprised that the kid was very tender with a satisfying taste. She had not eaten it before and her appetite grew quickly. She ate the meat and drank the strong beer, found it raw but there was neither coffee nor water. The fiery beans she left to others.

Pedro Rojas joined them, backed up Avery's claim that Angela was his niece, gorged himself in haste, then dashed back to spell Tony at guarding the animals and packs which, left alone, would be rifled by the curious. Mollified, Dolores went to change to a riding costume.

When the bowls were empty, the tortillas gone, Avery went around the bar and loaded a sack with liquor, then ushered Angela back to the street.

Tony passed them on his way to the cantina. Men watched their progress, turned about and followed. Avery walked casually, pausing often to exchange words with both civilians and the military, seemingly undisturbed by the attention they were drawing. It took most of an hour to laze the two blocks to the barn and corral.

By the time they reached it Tony had returned, Dolores had come by some back route and the horses were ready for travel except to tie on the sack of liquor. The party mounted and walked the string slowly into the afternoon heat. A curious group had gathered outside the runway and studied the loaded animals critically, but now all that were not ridden wore packs and the heavy gold had been distributed among them all so that none carried a burden that looked unusually heavy, and the audience lost interest. Avery Christian led off south on the trail toward the tumble of mountains without hindrance. But he did not relax the tension that his façade of amiable unconcern kept hidden until they were miles below the town. Then his relief expressed itself in a long dissertation on Mexico to Angela.

'Two Sierra ranges parallel to each other across the country, the southern one fairly gentle, clothed in luxuriant jungle. The Sierra de la Madera del Norte is the opposite. Barren in spots, an endless tumult of jagged canyons thousands of feet deep between austere rocky faces, cruel even in the foliage growing there, a land for the foolhardy peopled by

Indians, some demoralized and beaten, hiding in remote places, some as savage as any known.

'Three tribes call the mountains home. On the high timbered mesas of the eastern slope is the sorry remnant of the Tarahumares, once a numerous people. They were among the first to be made slaves by the early Spaniard invaders, brutally forced to work the rich gold mines and the vast haciendas in the lush canyon valleys. West of them are the Opathas, no longer a viable tribe. Both are decimated and their blood lines mixed, their language forgotten, only a very few Indios left.

'Beyond them, down the western slope is Yaqui country. Cousins of the Apache, these are proud and fierce, an independent force whom neither the Spaniards nor later the Mexicans had ever conquered.

'This Sierra is a world forgotten by history for over two hundred years. A silent, brooding, haunted land that was once the most productive area of Mexico. Its mines disgorged more gold and silver than any other section of North America. The ranches were a cornucopia of grain and fruit and cattle. Every pueblo boasted a solid stone church.

'All of that was before the slaves rebelled, killed the ranchers, closed the mines, ran out the priests who had owned the mines and funneled their wealth into the religious order. Ironically the government had completed the destruction by forbidding the church to own mines.

'With sufficient warning the padres hid the metals already above ground, blocked and concealed the mine entrances, prepared maps to relocate them if the ban was ever lifted, concealed those and abandoned their Indian neophytes. Those hapless, degraded people fell easy prey to Apaches raiding from the north down into the mountains to re-enslave them.'

As Avery Christian described the history, taking his niece into the appalling, apparently empty desolation, Angela felt its oppression reach out for her as they approached the foothills. In this company the Sierra would be far worse than the Superstitions, and foreboding filled her.

They camped at dusk some twenty miles south of Agua

Prieta and at daylight pressed on. The day and her mood worsened. The carefree attitude with which Avery and the Rojas had entered Mexico had deteriorated when they came to Agua Prieta and now continued the decline. The cousins were clearly nervous and watchful, constantly scanning the land ahead, to the sides, behind, and even Avery rode with his rifle out of the boot, across his saddle.

Finally she said, 'What is it you're afraid of here? You said it would be safe south of the line?'

'Safe from posses it is, and Janos will be safe.' He gave her a broad wink as reassurance. 'It's between here and there we need to take care. This country bubbles with revolutions that have torn it apart, turned a lot of otherwise harmless people into starving bandits with empty bellies they'd want to fill from our packs if we ran into them, and I don't mean to let them within smelling distance of my money.'

'My money.' She said it silently to herself. Not our money as he had referred to it before. An unaccountable chill touched her. He could be so charming, could make her feel important, but now he put this claim between them. Something worried her about the way he seemed to reflect like a mirror without letting her see into him. She wondered if it hid some mystery of his character he did not want her to learn.

And every time her horse set down a hoof it took her farther from those who had helped until she was, yes . . kidnapped.

Chapter Thirteen

Emile Chavez rode into Tombstone leisurely. No one hurried in the noon sun unless he were being chased. On Allen Street he saw Wyatt Earp and two of his brothers lounging in the shaded doorway of the Oriental Saloon yarning with Doc Holliday. The Tucson editor was well known in the town and the Earps waved him down, invited him inside for a drink.

Since Virgil Earp was marshal Chavez thought he might, without asking, pick up the information he wanted. He got down, trailed the men through the batwings and joined them in the line along the bar. The room was filled and talk was flowing, but if the quartet knew anything of Eaton's telegrams or of a search for Hannibal Heyes, Kid Curry, a string of horses brought through by three men and a blonde girl they were being close mouthed about it. Eaton would surely have alerted the law here to the stolen fortune in gold and there should be gossip buzzing through the room, but though he listened for an hour Chavez heard no whisper of any of it. Puzzled, he left, mounted, walked his horse to the O.K. Corral and livery, unsaddled and left the animal. From there he turned corners until he was in the alley that ran behind the *Epitaph* office, looked both ways, saw no one, and slipped through the rear door.

John Clum, the editor of that paper, stood at the type case breaking down a page. At sight of Chavez his eyes brightened with interest. He wiped his ink-blackened fingers on his stained canvas apron and bounced forward to shake hands.

'What did you do, fly?'

Chavez widened innocent eyes. 'How's that, Johnny?'

'Don't you know? Didn't Tucson get a wire from a Ross Eaton?'

'Not while I was there. I've been out on a story. What's breaking?'

'A big one.' Clum kneaded his hands happily. 'I'll give it to you if you promise to hold it until I publish. It's worth the deal, Emile.'

Chavez appeared to consider, watching his friend through narrowed eyes until he should be judged properly impressed, then he said mildly, 'I'll take a chance, your nose twitching like it is. What's your scoop?'

Clum sat down, flapping a hand at a second chair, wriggling in his as a town gossip prepares to spread her juicy story.

'The telegraph operator's in my pocket, gave me a copy of two wires right after Johnny Behan got the originals from Phoenix. They said Hannibal Heyes and Kid Curry had been captured but escaped and are presumed to be heading this way trying to get to Mexico.'

'You don't say.' Emile Chavez sounded convincingly astonished. 'What's the sheriff doing?'

'Going crazy.' Clum shook with soundless laughter. 'Has posses out all along the border trying to seal it off. Hell, there aren't enough men in the territory to cover all the crossings. Keep listening. The boys have a gang again, possibly a girl and probably her uncle, Avery Christian, a Mexican-loving road agent, and some others. This Eaton is an express agent and they hoodwinked him out of fifty thousand dollars Wells Fargo money he'd recovered in the Superstitions.'

Looking bemused, Chavez said, 'Funny I didn't hear it in the Oriental. Not a whisper.'

Clum cawed. 'You bet you didn't. There's a mint worth of rewards up for all of them and anybody who can collect it can retire. The locals are in and out of town, keeping mum, scratching their heads figuring where to look.'

'That's typical. What does Behan think?'

'He sent Billy Breakenridge, his deputy, west toward the San Pedro and took another bunch down to Skeleton Canyon to close the San Luis pass. But they're too late.'

'So?'

'They were both out hunting somebody else when the wires came and the telegraph operator sat on the news two days until they got home.'

Chavez relaxed against the chair, stretching his legs, his ankles crossed indolently. 'It's more than a two-day ride from Phoenix. The birds must still be north of the line.'

'No, they are not.' Clum's face was eager with more disclosures to make and he leaned forward, tapping a finger against Chavez' chest. 'I saw them go through. Not Heyes and Curry but Christian, a girl and two hombres. But I hadn't seen the wires at the time and didn't know what I was looking at. They've made it to Mexico all right.'

Chavez showed astonishment. 'You mean they paraded through Tombstone?'

'Emile, Heyes and Curry are not stupid. I mean I spotted Tony Rojas on Tough Nut street. Generally he hangs close to his sister's cantina in Agua Prieta or at Janos in the Sierra where he comes from, and rustles a few cattle to shove north when his pesos run low. I wondered if he had some in the brush out of town and was looking for a buyer, so I mossied down to the livery, saddled up and rode east a way, poking around. I was back in a little draw when I heard harness and eased down to see who was there. It was Rojas with a pack horse hauling a load, heading toward Galeyville, and you know that part of the San Simon valley is a no man's land except for outlaws.

'To make it short I trailed along out of sight. Close to Galeyville he swung off toward Skeleton and joined the party, a cousin, Christian and a knockout of a girl with a string of saddled horses I figured were stolen. I watched them sling some mighty heavy packs on the animals and head for the canyon. That Wells Fargo gold, I'd say. It's through San Luis and long gone by now.'

Emile Chavez frowned, pinching his lower lip. 'Then why did Behan send Breakenridge the opposite way?'

John Clum spread his palms helplessly. 'They don't know I saw what I did. It was too near night to come home so I laid over in Galeyville until morning. By the time I got here the wires had come, the posses were gone and half the town was swarming over the country with their tongues hanging out.'

Chavez used a tone of deep envy. 'Story of the year and you've got me muzzled. Well . . . When do you go to press with it?'

Clum licked his lips and grinned. 'I'm holding until Behan comes in with his tail between his legs. I owe him one for sitting on a murder last month until it was all over the street. Now, what do you know?'

Chavez sat exchanging newspaper chat for an hour to keep Clum's quick suspicion asleep, then departed by the rear door. That drew a sharp question as to what he was hiding from, where he was going.

'Over to Contention,' Chavez lied, 'and I just don't want to get tied up talking any longer. Shoot me a wire when I can print.'

He bought a bottle for Heyes and Curry and himself and rode east until he cut the print of the barred horseshoe to be certain there was not a coincidence in the party Clum had seen. He had been long enough in his profession to know coincidences were not infrequent and this was no time to blunder. Then he headed back toward the partners.

He did not as he had said find them that day. Night overtook him and he made a hungry, dark camp that would not attract a posse prowling the area.

Hannibal Heyes and Kid Curry watched the road to Tombstone until they could no longer see it. Three times groups of a few men rode by, searching the ground for tracks turning off.

'He's not coming,' Curry fretted. 'And he's told those jaspers where he thinks we are to claim the rewards. We'd better light out of here now.'

'He couldn't get the rewards unless he took us in himself. He'd get himself shot if someone else finds us and he tried to cut in. And with all the traffic I'd as soon stay here until they lose interest in this area. Kid, maybe Ross Eaton doped out that Chavez let us out of Phoenix and wired an all points for the three of us. He could be in jail himself.'

'Happy thoughts you have. I feel like a sitting duck.'

'If a duck stays quiet enough it can be missed. Grab some sleep and I'll take lookout until midnight.'

They had seen no other posses by nine in the morning but tension was building, uncertainty making even Hannibal Heyes jumpy whenever an animal noise broke the quiet, yet they knew the must sit the day out in the hot rocks fighting thirst because the canteens were nearly empty.

'What's that?' Curry straightened suddenly. 'You hear whistling?'

Heyes parted the brush before him and craned to see the

road. 'Horseman. One. Looks like, yeah, our editor. I wonder what it takes to make him move faster than a turtle.' He laid a hand on Curry's arm as the Kid started to his feet. 'Let him go on just in case he brought troops.'

Emile Chavez' horse walked sleepily, head bobbing in the mounting heat. Heyes and Curry waited fifteen minutes, saw no one following, returned to their horses and picked a way after him through the brush, not trusting the open road.

The boys had moved a mile from where Chavez had left them and they found him stretched on the creek bank, hat over his face, dozing. They watered their animals and filled the canteens before he heard them and roused, sat up with a melancholy smile.

'Do I have the correct impression that you lacked faith and feared I would abandon my research in favor of a quick buck for your hides? Shame. There's so much more of fascination to a reader yet to unfold. Did anyone in hot pursuit pass by your burrow?'

'Several,' Heyes told him. 'Suppose you unfold whatever you found out.'

The mock melancholy vanished in a pleased chortle. Chavez quoted Clum's words, told of his reconnaissance and finished on a puzzled note. 'One odd point. Ross Eaton did not include my name in his report of your escape. Would it be that he was embarrassed, or didn't he guess my part, or did we rattle that cool head for once?'

Kid Curry groaned. 'So he's laying the whole play on us. Hannibal, you know what's coming next? We're going to have Lom Trevors breathing smoke and fire right on our necks if we don't dive for Mexico pronto.'

'Uh-huh, and stickler that he is he'll cross over as quick as Eaton this time. We have to get that gold first.'

Emile Chavez' ears picked up at the name. 'Who is Lom Trevors?'

Heyes wished heartily that Curry had kept quiet but it was too late. 'Just another sheriff. Never mind. Let's move. Where do we pick up that trail?'

'We don't right away. Johnny Behan has the pass it goes through blocked now. We'll push south from here into

Mexico, then turn east and go direct to Agua Prieta. I know who they are now and where they're going.'

'That's dandy.' Curry's mouth turned down. 'If we don't trip over a posse first.'

Chavez was up, reaching for his bridle, saying over his shoulder, 'I'll scout ahead and give them a yell like I want to ask if they've found any sign if any turn up. You stay in hearing distance.'

They rode and for once Chavez set a smart pace. It was only half a day to the border down the San Pedro and Heyes puzzled that the others had not taken this shorter route. He discovered why when they got there. There was no real pass over the ragged hills and the horses could not have carried the gold across the steep climb except in a series of relays, a time-consuming process during which they could have been intercepted. Even traveling as light as the three were much of the barrier had to be crossed on foot, the horses led. But by night it was behind them and there had been no challenges, no pursuit. The next afternoon they were in Agua Prieta.

Here too the editor was known, nodded to on the street by men whom Heyes and Curry marked as villainous, dregs of the outlaws, yet Emile Chavez saluted them with his enigmatic smile and casual wave. The partners cocked an eye to each other in an unspoken question whether he was as undercover a member of their late profession as Ross Eaton was a cop. If so he must be even more successful than they had been, since Eaton accepted him at face value. It gave them both a cold chill because also, if Chavez had a criminal record and Lom Trevors did catch up he would hold them guilty by association. Heyes offered an almost imperceptible shrug. They could not separate themselves from him until they recovered the gold and rescued Angela Christian.

They followed his lead, dismounting before the cantina, ground reining the horses, trailing into the dim room. A squat, pockmarked Mexican behind the bar spread a grin, exhibiting a mouthful of gold teeth, and hailed Chavez in a rattle of Spanish.

'Hiyah, amigo, long time since you visit here.'

Chavez ambled to the counter and stood rocking idly from toes to heels, his language soft and fluent. 'Tequila for three, Manuel, and where's your gorgeous little sister?'

The Mexican's smile wiped away. His black eyes raked Heyes and Curry, then dropped to the shot glasses he set out and the brown clay jug he poured from. He said nothing.

'Meet Thaddeus Jones and Joshua Smith,' Chavez added. 'They're safe.'

The man was doubtful. 'What you want with Dolores this time?'

'Same as last. My nose itches.'

Manuel looked again at Heyes and Curry, hunched his thick shoulders to his ears, then mopped busily at the bar. 'You missed her by a little. Yesterday her good friend came with Tony and Pedro. She left the cantina to me for a time and went with them south to Janos in the mountains.'

Chavez spooned salt into the crook of his thumb and forefinger, licked it, tossed his tequila after it and said conversationally, 'Her friend Avery Christian?'

'Yes.' Manuel's forehead creased in a frown. 'He brought with him one he said is his niece, but I think Dolores doubted.'

'She needn't worry, Angela is a real niece, his brother's orphan.'

The cloud left the Mexican's face and he sighed. 'You relieve me, amigo, and for this niece's sake I hope Dolores now believes.'

'I'll tell her when I see her.' Chavez slid a coin across the counter. 'Hasta la vista.'

They left the Mexican looking disappointed that they had not stayed to eat, but chillis in the hot mid-afternoon did not appeal.

Outside Hannibal Heyes asked, 'Another Rojas?'

'One of many.' Chavez was amused. 'Theirs is an exceedingly fertile family. Tribe, you might say.'

The way south, no longer a road but a burro track, took them through country that changed quickly, through the valley of the Moctezume river, which would join the Yaqui and wind to the sea, then climbing into barren, wild foothills.

The village was larger than Heyes and Curry had expected, with a decaying church, its scaling dobe plaster showing crumbling rock construction probably three or more hundred years old. It faced a dirt plaza churned by many bare feet and a haphazard cluster of perhaps twenty mud and thatch huts. Scrawny dogs yapped and ran at them. Big-eyed naked children scattered to hide in the huts as dark men with much Indian blood spilled out and watched the arrival like a wall around the riders.

From the most pretentious structure one a head taller than the rest stalked out, shrugging into a long black coat greening with age.

'The jefe. Head man,' Chavez identified him, sweeping off his hat in salute. 'He knows me.'

'Oh no . . . He knows us too.' Kid Curry sounded strangled.

The man stopped ten feet away, looking up, shading his eyes with a hand, his mouth working in surprise. There was no mistaking the flat moon face with the knife scar from the corner of his right eye that crossed the fleshy cheek diagonally to lift the wide mouth in a twisting sneer. He had been a sometime hanger-on of the Hole in the Wall gang known only as Mex Quent, a clumsy outlaw. Heyes had been relieved when he got lost after a minor train robbery and assumed he had been shot or captured, and had never associated him with this or any other village.

He came closer, trying for a warm smile but it looked like a menacing grimace. In the States he had spoken broken English but here he was more comfortable in his native tongue.

'Senor Chavez, I am honored, and more so that you bring my old friends. Welcome to Janos.'

'Uh-huh,' Curry said. 'Where'd you drop from, Quent?'

The man drew himself up in a show of dignity. 'I did not drop, Kid. This is my home, my village, these are my people I have come back to. You are looking for a sanctuary? You have found it. No one can take you from here without my permission.'

Since the Mexican did not know the status of the amnesty the offer sounded generous enough, but Hannibal Heyes caught the thinly veiled threat that permission might not be granted if protection money was not paid. But that would not be mentioned until Quent ferreted out what the traffic would bear.

'Thanks,' he said. 'We would like to lite a spell but your people don't seem too friendly.'

'They will be when I explain. Step down and come out of the sun, to my house. It is yours.' He raised a yell that brought three half-grown boys out of the huts.

The partners and Chavez dismounted and the boys came to lead the horses away. Heyes watched after them, reluctant. If Mex Quent was harboring Avery Christian and the girl and knew about the gold they might need the animals in a hurry. But at the moment he would take his cue from the Tucson editor until he had a clearer idea of the score.

The jefe took them to the shade of the ramada built against his hut, furnished with a table and chairs, and left them to go inside. Chavez scratched the side of his nose as if it truly itched.

'You too have a wide acquaintance among dubious characters. Fortunately they titillate my readers, they're good copy.'

Heyes was guarded. 'What do you know about this one?'

'His name is Quenten Rojas. He's father to Dolores, Manuel and Tony and he runs this neck of the hills. Smuggler, killer, opportunist. I'm sorry he knows you. That may give us trouble getting information on Angela. We'll probably have to buy it.'

Before the boys could comment on the tribute Mex Quent should be expected to demand for information on which direction was north, the man was back, juggling a skin of mescal, drinking gourds and a clay cup holding a handful of small, crooked cigars rolled of strong, rank, black native tobacco. Behind him a fat woman brought a goat-meat stew, tortillas and frijoles.

She retired to let the men eat. Rojas dug into the stew with dirty fingers, licking them as he chewed each bite, simultaneously twisting tortillas one-handed to shovel beans into his mouth alternately with the goat.

Hannibal Heyes' and Kid Curry's hearty appetites dissolved like mist but Emile Chavez placidly followed the host's example and the boys thought it politic not to give offense, counting on the cactus liquor to disinfect the food.

Rojas' jaws worked steadily, leaving no time for speech until the vessels were cleaned. Then he poured more mescal and offered cigars around the table. When those were burning, as hot to the tongue as straight peppers, his scarred mouth climbed higher toward the drawn down eye in a caricature of a smile.

'Good to have old friends around the board again. Heyes, Kid, the States got too hot this time? You must have made a big strike. How much?'

'Wrong guess.' Chavez chuckled. 'They're helping me run down a story lead. I want to talk to Avery Christian.'

Mex Quent put on a show of quick dismay, spreading his hands, displaying them empty. 'My son-in-law? Why look for him here? I haven't seen him in months.'

'That's odd. He came through Agua Prieta with his niece, two of your family and picked up Dolores. They said they were coming here.' Chavez sounded no more than mildly puzzled. 'One of them rode a horse with a barred shoe and we last saw it a little out of town . . . Do I infer that Dolores and Avery got married?'

'At last, yes. And he has not been in Janos since. Perhaps they continued south without stopping.'

'Could be. His niece is interested in mountains, maybe she wants to see the country. So we'd better be on our way if we're going to locate her. Where did the kids take our horses?'

'To the village corral, just down this path.' Quent grimaced again. 'I would show you except that after I have eaten well I need the siesta. When you have found Dolores come for a longer visit.'

They left him ambling toward a hammock slung under the ramada thatch roof and walked the length of the crooked path between the irregularly set houses. As promised the mounts dozed in the shade of the pole corral built around a spreading tree and they took them south out of Janos at a run calculated to leave the impression they were hurrying after the Mexican girl.

In five miles they saw no barred hoofprint, the sun had set and it would soon be dark. Heyes pulled up, uncertain.

'I'd say Quent was lying in his teeth if I'd seen another horse except the crow bait in that fence, or a building big enough to hold one. Where did we lose those people?'

'Behind us.' Chavez was amused, stepping out of his saddle. 'Let's rest here until dark and go back.'

'You think they're out in the bush waiting for night to go in again?'

Heyes and Curry got down, drank from the canteens to put out the fire in their stomachs, increasingly worried at where Angela Christian could be. Chavez showed no such concern.

'The Janos church,' he said without emphasis, 'is old Spanish, built by Indian slaves when labor cost nothing and stone was free. They're more elaborate than they look from outside. Big heavy doors, two story naves and they all have a cavernous vault underground with an inside stairway wide enough that a horse could crowd down. The old priests stored their mined and milled metal there until they had enough to ship on a burro train to the coast for transport to Spain. There can be other uses for that space.'

'Do tell.' Kid Curry began to smile. 'It ought to be nice and cool down there too. Would there be a back way in?'

Emile Chavez rolled a cigarette, his gaze thoughtful, far away. 'Considered more as a back way out. Hidden for two reasons. With only a few priests at a given center and a high slave population it was safer to have an escape route in case of revolt. Also, being able to disappear into the church and reappear somewhere else they hadn't been seen moving to, helped the superstition that they had mystic powers. There'll be a tunnel under Janos that comes up in the house where the priests lived.'

'That doesn't add up,' Curry protested. 'If the slaves built everything they'd know about the tunnel.'

'Not if they were disposed of when the work was complete

and a different tribe brought in. They were saving souls, not lives.'

'Oh.'

Hannibal Heyes wanted to know how to find the right house that concealed the entrance.

'Only other stone building around. It's coated with 'dobe like the rest, but there's one, set apart, that's peeled and shows rock behind the mud. Say a thousand feet behind the church.'

'Beautiful. Can horses get through the tunnel?'

'Yes. But not up through the trapdoor into the house.'

Heyes pictured the layout and what they would have to do. 'Say then that Avery, the two girls and the Rojas men are in the vault with the gold and their animals. When it's good dark we leave our horses at the house, use the tunnel and surprise everybody. We can take the prisoners, tie them in saddles, load up the train, but we'll have to go out through the front. If I know Quent he'll have everybody in town on the roofs with guns waiting in case we didn't fall for his stall. We'll have Avery and Dolores and the Rojas. Four hostages. I wonder if Quent would take a chance on getting his daughter killed to keep us from riding out.'

Kid Curry laughed and flipped his gun. 'He'll hold the fire if we have him too. Mex likes his neck and a whole hide.'

'Uh-huh. First then we pick him up before he knows we're back, knock him on the head to keep him from yelling and lug him down with us.'

They talked until the shadows were dense and there was starlight to see by but no moon, then retraced the path, circling around the huts to the stone houses. There Heyes and Curry left Chavez with the horses, left their spurs so they would make no noise to wake the dogs, and slipped through the midnight to Quent Rojas' house.

It was not large and the door stood open for what air stirred. Inside they listened for breathing, heard loud snores from a second room and prowled toward the sound. In the dim glow through a window with no glass they made out a form too gross to be the Mexican outlaw and searched further. Rojas was not in the building. Heyes touched Curry's arm and they left, returned to Chavez with the word that that part of the plan had miscarried. It left a loose end that neither liked.

'Imagining myself in his situation,' the editor suggested. 'My siesta would have been short. I'd have gone to the church with the warning we were in the area and to stay underground. I believe I would have remained to feast on the sight of so many bright coins and to bargain with Avery for a share. Let's not spook until we know.'

More and more the boys approved of the man's grasp of probabilities. They led their three horses through the house door, heads dropped and the withers just missing the head-frame. Chavez struck a match, shielded the light from the openings and moved with Heyes across the room. The floor was paved with stone set without mortar, almost identical, and even if they were only two inches thick they would be heavy. But in a corner one square was split across the center by a ragged break. Heyes used his knife point to pry into the crack. One side of the slab lifted with ease. He pulled on it and it tipped, hinged at the square corners. Wide open it gave a space even a portly man could climb through and below there was a dark pit. Another match showed steep stairs. Heyes stepped down.

Kid Curry said sharply, 'Snakes?'

'No,' Chavez told him. 'It's sealed up and bone dry. Go ahead.'

The dust of ages was inches thick on the descending stone flight, on the tunnel floor at the bottom. There they could stand upright.

'Give me the lead,' Curry said softly, afraid of sound carrying down the passage. 'Quent won't try to draw on me if he's there. He knows better.'

The blackness was all but solid, only gravity telling what was up and down. Trailing their fingers against the wall to guide them the three felt their way, their movement muffled by the dust. Counting steps they judged they were midway of the tunnel when it turned gently. There was light at the far end, a dull glow that did not enter the passage more than a foot.

Both Chavez and Heyes walked with their short guns in their hands but Curry's hung in the holster. At the mouth where the vault opened Curry stopped the others, edging forward to see the room. It was as wide as a barn, ten feet high, lighted by torches set in wall brackets. He studied it a moment then backed against Heyes, whispering.

'All present and accounted for. Our blonde white as a ghost, looks like she wants to cry. A gal I take to be Dolores with an arm around her talking a blue streak, over across the room out of the way. This you should see, Quent, two that must be the Rojas boys and one that has to be Avery, squatted around a blanket on the floor shooting crap with a stack of gold each. Horses, gear beyond and money bags against the far wall. You ready to go?'

'A second,' Heyes whispered. 'Take it slow until we're seen. Chavez, the Mexican girl will have a knife or a gun in her garter. You throw down on her and we'll hit the men. Now.'

Kid Curry slid through the opening and to the side without attracting attention. Heyes followed, stopped where he would not block Emile Chavez. The editor, behind the partners the length of the tunnel, inhaling the dust their feet had set afloat, stepped into the vault and sneezed.

Dolores spun away from Angela, saw the intruders and screamed, doubled over to fight her skirt and reach her weapon. Chavez fired into the floor at her feet. The reverberation drowned other shouts as the dice players whipped around. Kid Curry's call was high enough to hear.

'Quent. Here.'

One second his hands hung at his sides. In the next fraction his gun was steady on the Mexican, also covering Avery Christian just beyond him. Hannibal Heyes' barrel swung between the Rojas boys where they squatted two feet apart. The men around the blanket froze, then very carefully lifted their hands.

Chavez' shot did not stop Dolores more than a blink of time. Like a tiger she jumped, dragging Angela to her feet, snapping her in front as a shield, bent again to her hem. It took time enough that Chavez' long jump reached her and he wrapped one arm around her waist, wheeled her off her feet and tore her lose from the blonde girl. He held her, kicking, fighting, touching the muzzle of his gun against her ear, prodding hard enough to tip her head until she took notice. She only kicked harder, cursing in Spanish using phrases Chavez was startled that even a bar girl knew.

Angela Christian had been flung aside, caught her balance and stood with both hands clasped against her face, the large deep blue eyes twice their normal size and almost black.

'Angela.' Chavez was sharp to catch her attention. She was a moment reacting, then he went on. 'Hike up Dolores' skirts and take the weapon she has against her leg. Then feel over her and see if she has any others, maybe in her blouse on that necklace.'

The stunned, slanted eyes turned abruptly hot and aware. Angela was thorough, dodging the flying heels. She found the derringer in a small garter holster, a thin, wicked knife sheathed in a jeweled scabbard suspended between the breasts. Her own little gun that she had worn into the Superstitions had disappeared when Avery had taken her from the brakes and she appropriated the derringer, dropped the knife into Chavez' pocket.

'Oh, I'm glad, so glad you came. So glad to see you.' She kept repeating the words, almost a chant, until she stepped away, her face radiant now, color returning, growing to a flush that made her lovelier yet.

Chavez dropped her a long wink. 'Now if we may take liberties, unfasten her petticoat, tear some strips of it, catch those ankles and immobilize them.'

The dark girl thrashed in Chavez' arm, clawed behind her for his face, could not reach it, grabbed a long fingered handful of Angela's pale hair and shook the head viciously. Emile Chavez, finding his gun was no deterrent, holstered it, used the freed hand to take Dolores' wrist and twist. Angela gave no heed to the hair pulling. Her hands were busy beneath the full skirt again, finding the tie at the waist, pulling it open to yank the petticoat down past first one flailing leg, then the other. When the linen would not tear she dug for the knife, sliced the cloth, then rent it, tied a slip knot and captured the ankles one at a time, binding them tight together. Chavez set the girl on her feet, drew the arms behind her and held them while Angela wound another strip around them, pulled it twice between the wrists and knotted it, wrapped the long ends around the waist and knotted it again in front.

Across the wide vault no one was watching the action of the girls and Chavez. Quent Rojas had thrown one glance that way, then concentrated on Hannibal Heyes and Kid Curry. After the first startled second while he looked at the guns his mouth warped and he laughed aloud as if delighted to see the men.

'Hiyah, boys.' It was a welcoming shout. The lie came smoothly. 'Look who blew in a half hour after you rode out.' The voice dropped, conspiratorial. 'Avery, meet Hannibal Heyes and Kid Curry. All in the family.' He gestured around the blanket, making introductions. 'Avery Christian, my girl's husband. My son Tony, and that's my nephew Pedro. Get yourselves a stack of chips and join the game. Here, I'll get them.'

He twisted to scramble up as though that were expected. Kid Curry put a shot on either side of him, two inches from the hands that had swept toward the guns at his hips.

'Sit quiet, Quent. I might get jumpy.'

Quenton Rojas settled back with care and sounded aggrieved. 'What about Kid? Look over there what Avery brought us, all out of Wells Fargo. Come on, we'll cut you in equal for old times' sake.'

'You will?'

The temptation in Curry's tone chilled Heyes. Curry with a gun in his hand was to be reckoned with. He said hurriedly, 'Kid. Lom's coming. Be sure of that.'

'Uh.' Curry swallowed. 'No thanks, Quent. Nice of you though.'

Avery Christian took his cue from the Mexican, looked impressed and gingerly extended a hand, easy charm in his voice. 'Heyes and Curry? I'm proud to meet you. Be proud to have you with us. There's enough here for all of us.'

Intent on the two train robbers none of the four around the blanket had noticed Emile Chavez lift the derringer from Angela's holster, fold it into her hand and indicate that she should watch over the dark, spitting girl sitting on the stone floor, then drift along the wall to where saddles and gear were ranged. Looping the coils of lariat over an arm he ambled behind Avery Christian, knocked him out with his gun butt then moved to do the same to the three Rojas men, his smile tender and amused.

Heyes and Curry shot their guns home, caught the coils Chavez tossed them, bound the unconscious figures hand and foot, then gave their attention to the horses. When they were saddled, the packs cinched in place, they loaded the unopened gold bags in the pouches. Chavez showing the way, he and Curry each led a horse to the arch and the stone stairs that went up to the church nave. It took time, cajoling, sometimes a swat on a rump to make the animals climb the twenty feet into the high vaulted center of the old building. They secured the first two and went back for others.

Hannibal Heyes had gathered up the coins scattered around the blanket, searched the pockets of the players and found more, and stowed them in the bags they had been poured from. That finished, he joined Chavez and Curry in moving the train above ground. One after another the bound men woke, yelled, swore, struggled on the stone floor helplessly.

When the last of the animals was in the nave, strung together on a lead line where there was headroom to mount and ride through the high, heavy double doors that opened on the plaza, the three went below again.

'Should be near daylight,' Heyes said. 'We ought to be away from here before the town wakes up and we'd have to fight our way out. Let's get some hostages up there and clear out.'

'All of them?' Curry was aghast. 'That's a lot of weight to load across those animals.'

'Not all. Only Dolores and her daddy, the jefe. If anybody's up and watching I think they wouldn't want those two hit by a stray bullet.'

'Not Avery Christian?' Chavez said in mock horror. 'Ross Eaton will want him to jail.'

'Let him come after him,' Heyes said. 'He's the law man.

If we take his gold back that's enough.'

All three had walked to where Dolores still squirmed and screeched and Angela stood out of reach, her eyes and her gun focused intently on the captive, her body straight and rigid. Emile Chavez moved into her sight slowly, not to startle her, coughed for attention.

When she glanced at him he reached for the derringer, prying her white fingers loose from it.

'A very good job, my dear. I'll relieve you now.' The voice was a soothing purr.

Angela jumped as if a trance had broken, turned and saw Heyes and Curry and her face lighted again. Her smile spread, the cheeks stiff at first, then relaxing into softness. Hannibal Heyes was closer. She threw her arms wide and lunged against him, wrapping him in a tight grip, jumping off her toes to kiss him squarely. Because she was too short it was a peck only but it burned on his lips like sweet fire. Before he recovered enough to hold her she swung to Kid Curry, kissing him the same, but alerted by Heyes' kiss the Kid caught her, bent his head and held her mouth for seconds. She broke loose breathless, stepped back and laughed.

'I never knew I could be so glad to see anybody. You three.' She turned indignant. 'My uncle. I always thought he was wonderful. Then he kidnapped me and told me he had a right to the gold because Wells Fargo had ruined him. He had me believing it until we got here, though I had some suspicion. But this . . . this . . . ' she swept an arm around the vault. 'Why, he's plain craven. Can we get the money back where it belongs?'

Faces flaming, Heyes and Curry nodded. Heyes said, choking, 'Now you're all right that's the next job.' He suddenly remembered urgency. 'Chavez, chase out and bring our horses. The Kid and I will finish here.'

Not arguing, Emile Chavez swung toward the tunnel, snagged a torch out of a bracket in passing, and ran.

Kid Curry pointed out the rising stairs to Angela, made a shooing gesture, then stopped over Dolores, smiling, saying, 'You're going with us.' It took some moments to gag her as she still threw herself from side to side. 'Keep fussing, honey, and I'll have to clip you. We're running behind time.'

The black eyes hated him but she quieted. He lifted her in his arms and headed after Angela. Hannibal Heyes finally got a handkerchief fastened in Quent Rojas' mouth, put a hand between the tied legs, the other between one arm and the body and slung the man across his shoulders, draped around his neck, and sprinted for the steps, Avery Christian's bellows following.

In the time it had taken to subdue the hostages and bring everyone to the nave Emile Chavez had brought the horses. As Heyes reached the top the editor swung the big front doors wide and led the animals inside.

It took both Heyes and Curry to untie the dark girl's legs, set her astride Curry's horse and cinch her hands against the horn, tie the legs again to the stirrups. Then they boosted the Mexican jefe aboard Heyes' animal, secured him, and both partners mounted, holding the bodies close against them. Chavez had helped Angela into his saddle, passed the lead line to Heyes, then he lifted in a stirrup, eased his leg across and lowered himself to share the deep leather seat with the blonde.

Hannibal Heyes in the lead towing the loaded string, Emile Chavez and Angela behind, Curry with Dolores bringing up the rear they rode through the open door into the early dawn to the dim plaza.

Chapter Fourteen

The message that burned the wire from Sheriff Lom Trevors to Ross Eaton reached Tombstone before the Wells Fargo agent. If the two train robbers had escaped the Phoenix jail Trevors knew they would bolt for Mexico and Tombstone was the logical starting point for a search. He knew the boys of old, the turns their minds took, the pattern of their escapes, the sort of hiding places they would make for. The words on the yellow paper were imperative.

HOLD EVERYTHING ON HEYES CURRY FOR MY ARRIVAL FRIDAY. I'LL TRACK THEM TO PERDITION.

Ross Eaton, driving hard into town on Thursday afternoon, would have disregarded the demand except that by the time he had talked with Sheriff Billy Behan and editor John Clum and learned that part of the fugitive band had been seen, their direction ascertained, it was too late to resupply and head south that day. Further, when the Phoenix sheriff heard the men they were chasing were already across the line, he declared himself and his posse would return home since they would not cross the boundary. And Behan, with the same constriction on him, would not go out again. On the other hand Sheriff Lom Trevors of Porterville, whoever he was, sounded outraged enough to defy restrictions. Eaton spent the rest of the day provisioning for a party of two, wiring the Rurales garrison at Agua Prieta and poring over Behan's maps of the Sierra Madre del Norte.

Trevors routed him out of his hotel bed at dawn. He had caught a night train to Benson, rented a horse and plowed into Tombstone in a rage. Eaton liked what he saw, a big, strong-faced man who carried himself with proud confidence, spoke in a calm, resonant voice and announced he would have Hannibal Heyes' and Jeb Kid Curry's heads if it was his last act on earth.

Over breakfast together Eaton told Trevors he had an answer from the Rurales. Avery Christian and three Rojas people had taken a string of horses south and next day Emile Chavez and two gringo strangers had passed through in the same direction. The Mexican force agreed to place twenty men under Captain Alonzo Gomez in the field at Eaton's disposal.

Trevors would have been happier without them. Two men were less conspicuous on a chore like this, but he did not challenge the Wells Fargo agent's play. He made one concession to regularity, stopped at Behan's office on the way to the livery and laid his polished star squarely in the center of the battered desk. Then he and Ross Eaton rode hell bent for Skeleton Canyon and beyond.

Through the blistering day Ross Eaton, as hot under the skin as he was outside, told Trevors his version of the trip into the Superstitions, the recovery of the treasure, his new conviction that Heyes and Curry were working with Avery Christian, his lack of conclusion of how Angela Christian fitted in the gang.

'They're out of their skulls,' Trevors said with venomous quiet. 'And they've never used a woman before that I know of, but there can always be a first. What about this editor, is he one of them?'

'Not unless he's pulled the wool over my eyes for four years, and I'm not easy to fool. No, Chavez would tweak the Devil's nose to build a story and this is the biggest one that's fallen in his lap for a long time. He's all right but I'd like to choke him.'

In the fastest ride Trevors hoped he would ever make they came into Agua Prieta after sunset on the second day. Captain Gomez read the drawn faces, deplored the hard used horses, insisted the men take supper with him and sleep in the officers' quarters.

With the first difference between dark mountain and faintly lighter sky the three set out at the head of the column. Gomez warned that the Rojas tribe was as dangerous as Apaches and would take numbers to overcome. It was late when the troop approached Janos. Gomez refused a night entrance and Trevors and Eaton agreed to wait over, not knowing the village. They stopped a mile short of it, made a dark camp, Gomez posted a rotation of sentries and the Rurales stretched on the ground to sleep, the Captain soon lightly snoring.

Neither Ross Eaton nor Lom Trevors joined them. Eaton was kept keyed up by anticipation, the joyful picture of snatching back the twice lost gold, the greater pleasure of laying Avery Christian, Hannibal Heyes and Kid Curry by the heels and throwing the fear of God into Emile Chavez.

Lom Trevors was too troubled to relax. He could not decide what had possessed the partners to involve themselves in this caper. For months they had toed the line admirably, were well on their way to full pardon. He was personally hurt, betrayed, and even when he dragged them by the scruff of their collars before the Governor he knew he would lose prestige and shake the faith he and the Attorney General had placed in him. The churning thoughts fueled the anger in him until by force he schooled himself to rest. The next day he wanted all his energy and wit razor sharp.

At four o'clock the sentries on shift roused Captain Gomez. The Captain knew his people well and had less than full respect for the gringos with him. Such intense fury as he had seen in them the day before did not augur cool heads when they would be needed. He got his men up quietly and took them ahead on foot, leaving two to bring the horses closer but hold them back where their odor would not warn the dogs. Eighteen went in with him, clubbing those curs that did growl or rush them. In groups of three they passed from hut to hut, entering, confiscating firearms, warning the occupants that if they raised a noise or put their heads out they would be shot. When the place was unarmed and cowed Gomez sent the soldiers to the roofs surrounding the plaza, then returned to the horses, picked up his and rode back to the sleeping Americans. There would be light in an hour.

He called them awake, told them his preparations, explaining, 'There is no sign of your fugitives in Janos, Señors. Unless they have passed beyond it the only place they can be is in the church. I have that surrounded and the fear of God thrown into the villagers. We did not find the jefe either, who is a villain and my money says he is with Christian in the basement vault. We need only keep out of sight and wait to see who comes into the plaza.'

Ross Eaton rammed to his feet, roaring. 'Wait hell. I'm taking your troop and breaking in that place. It's a perfect trap and the surprise . . . ' His words trailed off at the ice suddenly in the Captain's eyes.

'A church is sacred in this land. It is sanctuary. Señor, you are not in command. You are in my country by courtesy only. You have no authority here.'

Lom Trevors closed his mouth abruptly. He had been on the verge of arguing for Eaton's action, and the mistake yawned before him like an abyss. He crowded down his impatience, his eagerness to face the train robbers who were mocking all he had done for them, growling.

'He's right, Eaton. I'm in a hurry too but let's not lose our heads this close to the quarry. Captain Gomez, the say-so is yours but let's get about it.'

Gomez did not relax. He had seen the flash spark in the sheriff's eyes before it was veiled and he said flatly, 'There will be no shooting by either of you. If the outlaws are so foolish as to attempt a fight my men on the roofs will fire back. Give me either your word or your guns.'

Fuming, the Americans accepted the order, mounted their horses that had been left for them and rode with Gomez to where the others were tied. They walked from there. The Captain could see in the dark or he knew the path by heart. Without a misstep he took them to the plaza, stopped for a word with his lieutenant who told them someone had recently taken three saddled horses in through the high church doors, then led Trevors and Eaton across to the front corner of the dark building.

They waited there in the shadow. A fingernail of light grew along the ragged crest of the eastern peaks. It widened, bringing the huts into relief against the sky but no figures showed on the roofs. The dusty, empty plaza became visible. Nothing moved there. Half an hour passed without sound. Ross Eaton looked at Trevors, jaw thrust forward and one eyebrow arched. Lom Trevors clenched his teeth, seeing futility in the wait, seeing the men he so wanted miles away and a long hard chase stretching before him. Captain Gomez touched their shoulders, cocked his head. Hinges made a soft creaking. Gomez touched their holsters in warning. The double doors swung wide, outward. Gomez drew them back around the corner. Hoofs clattered on the stone steps then fell silent in the dust as others took their place.

A horseman stepped his animal into view and the increasing light showed two men aboard, close enough to identify.

'Hannibal Heyes.' Trevors' whisper was a hiss against the two heads close to his.

'With the jefe as hostage. Tied on and gagged.' Gomez' soft slur, laughter in it.

Behind the riders came horses on a lead, some saddled, some wearing packs. Then two more figures mounted on the same animal.

'Chavez with Angela Christian.' Ross Eaton's voice trembled.

The end of the train appeared.

'Kid Curry.' Trevors said it through his teeth.

Gomez spoke through a low chuckle. 'Holding the jefe's beautiful daughter Dolores, who also is trussed and her mouth stopped. She will not be happy.'

They waited. The clatter on the steps had stopped. No one else rode into sight.

A low groan escaped Ross Eaton. 'No Avery Christian and Angela hasn't got a rope on her. She's in it up to her pretty neck.'

They were in the center of the plaza now, a ragged hundred foot square. It took all their will for Lom Trevors and Ross Eaton to keep from shouting at them to stop. They had drawn the breath for it when Captain Gomez lightly pushed them forward.

As they came out from the corner he called, laughing. 'Far enough, gentlemen. Look to the roofs.'

All heads went up. A fence of Rurales coralled the square, carbines bristling like spokes toward the hub of a wheel. The train pulled to a halt.

Emile Chavez' voice, interested but holding disappointment, crossed the small space. 'Ross?'

'I'm here. Dismount. Lift Angela down. Drop her side gun and yours. Step clear and raise your hands.'

As the editor put his leg over the saddle Lom Trevors controlled his urge to roar, called through stiff lips.

'Curry, touch your gun and you are dead. You're not fast enough for this. Get out of that leather. You, the blonde, empty his holster, throw as far as you can.'

Kid Curry moved with slow care, obeying, standing back from the horse, his hands shoulder high as Angela lifted his gun and hurled it away. Hannibal Heyes sat quiet, not turning his head, draining of hope. The way it had to look it was impossible that any law man could believe the truth. He did not dare move a muscle until he was told to.

Before the order came there was a flurry behind him. With Curry out of the saddle Dolores was in it alone. Tied to the stirrups as she was she kicked the animal's flank, her high heels as sharp as spurs. The haunches went down, then released like a spring in a bound past the horse ahead. The three men had advanced from the corner of the church, stalking, watchful. Captain Alonzo Gomez sprinted, caught the trailing rein and yanked the lunging horse in a tight circle that threw the dark girl off balance, slipping askew. Gallantly the Captain drew his short saber, cut the lower leg free, ducked under the animal's head to haul the girl upright, cut the other leg loose, then the thong around the horn. He pulled her down, hugged a flirtatious arm around her waist, his white teeth flashing. Dolores dropped her head, sank her teeth through the uniform sleeve and when he jerked back she broke away, running toward the church door. Ungallantly Captain Gomez tripped her second step and when she sprawled on her face sat on her back, tying the trailing petticoat strips at her ankles together again, then lifted her and kept hold of her, ignoring her as he returned to Eaton and Trevors, his smile dancing.

'She does excite a man. I think I will keep her.'

There was no room that morning in Ross Eaton or Lom Trevors for amusement. They had been diverted from the business of capture only until the girl was in hand again, then Trevors called sharply.

'Heyes, your turn. Get rid of your iron and down. Eaton, you'd better haul that jefe off so he doesn't bolt.'

Ross Eaton obliged, but when Quent Rojas was on the ground he tied him to the horse's foreleg where if he tried an escape he would be dragged under the hoofs.

There was time to look around the plaza then. The doorways of the huts were filled with the villagers, curious but wary under the carbines of the Rurales above them. Lom Trevors gave them a single glance, then beckoned the partners to him, standing his tallest, disdaining to touch his holstered gun, disdaining to speak as his smoldering eyes held them. The others gathered close. Ross Eaton was the first to break the long, strained silence.

'What did you do with Avery Christian?'

Emile Chavez answered, chuckling. 'Left him trussed up in the vault with two Rojas boys to do penance. He'll wait for you.'

The editor had played a game ever since they had gone into the Superstitions and Eaton's nerves were raw. 'Damn you,' he exploded. 'Damn Heyes and damn Curry. Now I know what you are. All three of you.' He shook a fist under Chavez' nose. 'You're with the Tucson Ring. You've played me for a sucker, conning me that this pair could be used to bring that gold out. All along you've meant to grab it for those parasites. I see through you now.'

Chavez raised the long, light lashes that screened his eyes, moved his head from side to side, sounding regretful. 'You know better than that, Ross. You've known me too long, too well, and you are not stupid. You'd have dug out a connection years ago. You're too upset to think. Cool down and listen. Trust me.'

'Trust you? I did trust you. I trusted Angela Christian. I thought she was an innocent victim. And I just saw her riding in your lap like she thought it was home. Right behind those horses that have fifty thousand dollars of Wells Fargo gold on them if it's all still together. She's as much a crook as the rest of you.'

Lom Trevors was silent, letting the tirade of accusation run on to nail down the exposure of Hannibal Heyes' and Kid Curry's guilty complicity, sick inside. They were old friends and those were the worst to lose.

A soft, urgent voice broke in as Angela crowded through to face Eaton. 'Ross, none of that is true. These men came here and put themselves in great danger to save me from my uncle, to take your precious gold from him and get it back to you. We were on our way back with hostages to see us safely across the border. I swear that's so.'

The agent looked anguished. This beautiful girl had wedged herself into his dreams, blinded him. He wrenched back a step, saying hoarsely, 'I wouldn't believe you on a mile of bibles. You're going to the States all right, and to prison until you're a hag. That's final.'

Scorn made her nostrils flare, her dark pupils swell, her voice a cutting edge. 'One truth my uncle told me. That people mean nothing to you. You used me. You knew it was not ore we were after, but gold. You did not tell me. You gave me no opportunity to say take it, it isn't mine. I am sorry for you, Ross Eaton.'

His mouth stretched to a tight, white line. 'Prison.' It was the only word he could manage.

'Prison.' Hannibal Heyes and Kid Curry echoed it under their breaths, their hearts sinking for themselves and Angela equally.

Emile Chavez and Captain Gomez exchanged a look across the group, the Captain pained at this possible waste of young womanhood, Chavez dropping him a wink.

'Captain.' The editor was airy. 'What authority do these Americans have in your bailiwick to make arrests?'

Gomez brightened. 'None at all, my friend.'

Ross Eaton roared at the Mexican. 'Then you arrest them and I'll get extradition. They are going back with me.'

'So? I know of no crime they have committed in my country. Should I drum up a false charge?'

To Heyes and Curry the words were hope to grasp at but both kept very quiet. It could still go either way. If Lom Trevors chose to call on the Governor's name, to suggest that man of stature, admired on both sides of the line, might appeal to a higher authority than a captain of Rurales, would Gomez surrender without a test? But Emile Chavez had not finished.

'Ross, you are opening yourself to a grave charge. Should I write an editorial on the arrogance of Wells Fargo condemning innocent people when you have no shred of proof that they are anything else, I don't often point out the power of the press so bluntly, but it is available.'

Ross Eaton's laugh was short, harsh. 'To you? It won't be. One proof I do have is that you are here in the middle of a gang of thieves and taking their part. Deny that.'

A sad smile lifted Chavez' mouth and he sighed, looking at Heyes and Curry. 'Difficult man.'

The blaze of the rising sun fell on Angela Christian's face, heightening the stormy color already there. She swung to Gomez.

'Captain, will you have my uncle brought up from the vault? And the Rojas boys?'

Gomez bowed, his smile wide again. 'For the Señorita, anything.'

He called six soldiers down from the roofs and sent them on the errand. Aside from the chatter from the hut doorways a strained silence hung in the plaza. Minutes later Avery Christian was walked out and brought to face his niece, the boys behind him showing worry. Christian looked over the gathering, mainly at Ross Eaton and Alonzo Gomez, his eyes shrewd. He smiled, handsome and confident. He was not wanted in Mexico and he knew the Captain was jealous of foreigners trying to usurp his authority. Gomez would not let Ross Eaton take him. Angela did not give him time to speak. She laid her hands on his shoulders, earnest, questioning eyes upturned.

'Uncle Avery, look at me. Really look at me. Am I pretty now?'

His easy smile widened. 'Pretty as they come, honey. I'm proud of you.'

Her words were even, unhurried. 'I won't be so for long if you don't admit the truth. Mr Eaton is convinced I knew what you and my father were doing and was helping you. He is determined to take me north to a prison. He says I'll stay there until I am old and ugly. Do you want that for me?'

Christian lost color. He raised his face to Eaton and read the furious determination. His voice came faint.

'No. No I don't. I guess I can stand it but you couldn't. Eaton, yes, I held up that stage but I didn't kill the driver. I held the team. We took the box, Eddie Brown and Bob Kenny and I. I gave them the slip and stashed the box where you found it. I don't know where Brown and Kenny are . . .'

'Killed by Apaches,' Eaton cut in. 'Your brother took them in with us.'

Christian shrugged. 'That's a laugh. Burt died there too. These boys and I,' he tipped his head toward the Rojas, 'trailed you out, picked up the gold when you went to sleep and took Angela with us. We left you three alone, guns, water. We didn't hurt you. She didn't know a thing until I told her next day. And she's been getting more scared of me ever since. That's all of it.'

Lom Trevors rumbled, his question coming on a long breath of relief. 'What about Heyes and Curry?'

'I never saw them until we hit Eaton's camp. And I sure didn't want to split with anybody more than the Rojas.'

Trevors closed his eyes, took off his hat, mopped his head, said weakly, 'You had the gold in the vault. When they took it did they say why?'

'I didn't believe it, knowing who they are, but they told Angela they'd return it to the damned express company.'

Hannibal Heyes and Kid Curry moved up on either side of the Porterville sheriff who looked ready to fall down. He tapped each on the arm, turned and walked away, turning his back to hide his face. The boys took Angela's hands, beaming on her, beginning to breathe again.

Kid Curry told her, 'I never had a guardian angel before. We really owe you.'

She was sober after the ordeal with her uncle. 'No you don't. It was I who owed you, for everything you did. I think I love you both.' For the second time she kissed them.

Ross Eaton was squabbling with Gomez again about possession of Heyes, Curry and Christian while Emile Chavez, hands shoved in his pockets, wandered aside, kicking at dust, bending unobtrusively to pick up the partners' hand guns, drop them into his jacket. He had retrieved both, unnoticed, when Eaton caught the blonde girl's kisses from the corner of his eye, broke away from Gomez and stormed to her. Heyes and Curry withdrew out of his range, backed against the horses, trying to make themselves as invisible as possible.

The turmoil within the Wells Fargo agent made him stutter as he apologized, explained, apologized to the stone faced Angela. Emile Chavez used the moment when Gomez stood alone with Dolores to idle to him.

'Captain,' the voice was low, conversational. 'You've had some favorable notice in the *Sun* from time to time. Would you like to see your name in headlines for your capture of Avery Christian today?' He read his answer in the eager face and continued. 'You aren't interested in Heyes and Curry. Can you get them out of this plaza quietly without being shot from the roofs?'

If the Mexican was startled he did not betray it. He threw a glare of dislike at Ross Eaton, raised his free hand high in a wave that changed to signals indicating that the partners were to be allowed safe passage out of the village, and received an answer in the lifting of the carbines to aim at the sky.

Emile Chavez ambled to Heyes and Curry at Eaton's back, palmed the guns into their holsters, his lashes down, a corner of his mouth tucked up, saying softly, 'Your two weeks wages will be waiting for you whenever you feel like dropping by for it.' He dug in a pocket and offered two silver dollars. 'Here's all I have on me at the moment. Captain Gomez finds you an embarrassment and has cleared a path.'

His slow walk had hardly halted. He moved on. Kid Curry gaped after him, glanced wide eyed at Hannibal Heyes, and the two ghosted to their mounts, swinging to the saddles with no quick movement, laid low along the necks on the side away from Eaton, then stayed not on the order of their leaving.

The abrupt pound of hoofs brought Ross Eaton around, slapping for his gun. Emile Chavez was in the way. Eaton shoved him, knocked him down. Chavez snatched at the gun hand, missed as it came up, but it did not matter. Angela Christian was on the agent, her full weight thrown across the arm, forcing it down.

In a swift look across their shoulders the partners saw the tangle as Eaton fought to break free. Then they were beyond the huts and in the open.

CHAPTER FIFTEEN

They headed south because south was downhill and Agua Prieta with its Rurales garrison was the opposite direction. A five-mile rush winded the horses and there was no sign of pursuit, and the boys pulled up to take stock.

Kid Curry asked wonderingly, 'How do you figure that joker anyway?'

Heyes took time before he answered. 'I've had him pegged half a dozen different ways but I think now he's just what he says he is. He wanted a story and he did what he had to to get it. Don't look at a gift horse to cheek its teeth.'

'I'd rather look at Angela. For the rest of my life. Did you see her come through, side us against Eaton? I thought he had the inside track until this morning when he showed his colors but he's clear out of the running now. As soon as I can find that girl again . . . '

'You?' Heyes was indignant. 'You'll have to get past me first, and she's out of your league. She knows a man with brains when she meets him.'

Curry smirked. 'You'll find out. Look at the record, who's always been first choice. You want to be best man at the wedding?'

They had seldom quarrelled and almost never over women, and this was a useless argument at the moment. There were miles and days ahead before they could find the blonde again and Heyes turned his thoughts to the immediate future, which was still precarious.

'The first thing we have to do is get back to the States. We can't stay out of the country more than a month or we lose the amnesty, so we've got to make a choice. We can't go through Skeleton Canyon or the way we came down, they're too close to Tucson and Johnny Behan, so it's east or west below the border.'

'Either one's a long way.' Kid Curry pictured the empty land. 'West it's all desert to Yuma, and the farther I stay away from the Hell Hole the easier I'll sleep. That prison is the worst man killer in the country.'

What else was well known and did not need mentioning was that the Mojave Apaches who lived along the Colorado where the Gila joined it were paid a hundred dollars each for every prisoner who attempted escape from the grim stone fortress on the bluff if they caught him and returned him. Any unfamiliar white man riding through there would be grabbed up on the chance that he was wanted.

The alternative was a hard eight hundred miles, across the spine of the Sierra, to the old capital of Chihuahua, then north to Cuidad Juarez, entering the States at El Paso. Even so the partners found that the more appealing route.

They had no provisions. What little food had remained had been shifted to the pack animals left at Janos, but that was not a worry. They had lived off the land time and again. Of more concern were Apache raiding parties looking for ponies at the few ranches they suffered to exist for the express purpose of breeding horses that they periodically stole. Those might hear a shot when the boys took game. But Heyes and Curry had played tag with Indians all over the west and three basic rules had stood them in good stead.

Never go to sleep at the edge of water. Never tie your mount near where you intended to bed down. An Indian could always smell out a horse farther than a white man, but someone burrowed in the rocks or brush was harder to locate. Third, sleep in turns with one always alert.

So they set the southern course. The mountain trail pinched and they rode single file through the Presa Angostura, the jaws of a winding passage, until it opened on the shore of a little lake, headwaters of the Yaqui. Following that they cut its tributary the Rio Papigochic, a tortuous rushing stream looping out of the high range, and there turned into the most brutal terrain as it climbed over the ridge. At Cuidad Guerrero they picked up the ancient treasure road where the burro trains had left their memory in deep ruts worn into the living rock by the thousands of small, sharp hoofs.

They ate fish from the rivers, not needing to use a gun that would echo through the canyons. Then Kid Curry made a prime find, a peccary, fifty pounds of fierce wild pig rooting in the rocky ground. It saw the man and made a dash for safety into its dark little hole of a cave, out of sight but it was cornered there. Curry stayed at the entrance, keeping it inside while Hayes gathered dry brush, built a fire at the mouth where heat and smoke was drawn down the hole. It was not long before the animal, pig-eyes blinded and snout choked, rushed out, onto the knives the partners held ready. They dined on the sweet fresh meat, took a day to jerk and smoke the rest, then rode on with a full larder.

But Angela Christian rose increasingly between them. The fair face and cascade of palest gold hair was even lovelier in retrospect and the fragile looking body that had withstood every rigor of the harsh trek through the Superstitions was a cause of growing wonder. She had kissed them both, however briefly and impulsively. They dreamed. And neither dream included the other. Kid Curry regretted that he had listened to Heyes, that he had not appropriated the Wells Fargo treasure and disappeared with the girl. Looking back he saw many opportunities, blanking out the fact that no one man could have managed it without being immediately run down by his partner and the avenging agent. It bred resentment that he did not conceal.

'You're doing great,' he complained, 'at getting us a fresh start. How much time have we put in and what do we have to show for it? Down here in the boondocks with two big dollars in our pockets and two weeks wages locked up in Tucson. It will be after the end of that year before we can show our faces anyplace near there. What do you expect me to support Angela on? We don't even rate a piece of that Wells Fargo reward after all the trouble we went to. Not even credit from Eaton.'

Hannibal Heyes too was less than happy. It was hard enough keeping the Kid on the straight and narrow. If it weren't that his own pardon hung on their both staying within the law he would have quit the partnership, go his own way, find Angela and talk her into waiting until his name was cleared. But he did not dare break with Curry until the pardon was granted and secure.

'So we're strapped again.' He was short. 'We've been there before often enough. There's no reason why when we hit El Paso we can't write to Chavez and ask him to get the wages to us. He owes us that much for winding up that story he's so hot to write.'

The rugged mountain passage did little to relieve the aggravations. They were out of tobacco when that would have been a solace and being denied even a smoke seemed the last indignity. When they reached Chihuahua the odors drifting out from restaurants they passed tantalized them further, but in the straightened circumstances they bought only a bag of coffee and one tobacco sack. There was still the four hundred mile haul straight north to the border.

When at last after three weeks in the saddle since Janos they reached the wide river and forded it from Juarez to the bustle of El Paso del Norte they were barely speaking.

Hannibal Heyes reined in and got down before the telegraph office, sent a collect wire to Sheriff Lom Trevors assuring him they were within the deadline for absence from the country, another to Emile Chavez, then he headed for the hotel.

Kid Curry broke a long silence with a yelp of protest when Heyes again dismounted. 'You're not throwing away money on a room here? What's wrong with the livery?'

Heyes rocked back on his heels, fists on his hips, explaining with what patience he could call on. 'Hotel lobbies usually have a newspaper lying around. Newspapers sometimes run notices of somebody looking to hire a hand. We need a job. Do you follow?'

'Oh. Yeah.'

Curry got down. At least the lobby would get them out of the sun for a few minutes. They tied the horses on the shady side of the sand street and tramped stiffly into the long dim hall. There was a desk with no one behind it and opposite that an arch into the saloon that gave off the sharp tang of whiskey neither had tasted in a month. Curry looked longingly toward the arch, squeezed his eyes shut against temptation and turned to the row of chairs along the wall.

Newspapers lay on most of the seats, some moderately fresh, most dogeared, torn, crumpled. Kid Curry picked up one of the newer, an El Paso edition, and skimmed the pages. He was halfway through when Hannibal Heyes tossed aside his first random choice and took another.

'Hey . . . ' The word made Curry jump. *Tucson Sun.* Heyes read the bold black headline aloud. 'Fifty thousand recovered by Wells Fargo . . . Here's Chavez' story.' He read the drop head, laughing for the first time in weeks. 'Editor accompanies search party on adventuresome expedition.'

Heyes sank into a chair reading the long, prominent column that crowded the usual advertising to half the page. Emile Chavez began with brief mentions of astonishing feats to be described in subsequent editions, wrote of the beautiful girl who had brought him the treasure map and insisted on making the dangerous trip into the forbidding mountains. He told of making up the escort to be led by an under-cover agent designated only as E., of the girl's father and his recruits who would play villainous roles before the end of the tale, of judiciously including two noted outlaws, S. and J., experienced in surviving and succeeding in regions and circumstances where the less knowledgeable must fail, men of a stamp who would predictably fall under the spell of the lady and raise themselves to heroic deeds to defend her and deliver her and the golden horde safely and honorably. He ended the instalment there, leaving a slavering readership impatient for more.

Kid Curry preened himself, polished his nails on his coat collar, saying dreamily, 'Not bad for a starter. It's a pretty good slant on us. By the time he's finished I'll be a shining knight to Angela.'

Heyes threw him a triumphant glance. 'That's just a sample of what he'll say when we've got the pardon and can give him an exclusive. But it doesn't feed us now.'

He followed down the columns of ads and notices hoping

a trail drive might be announced by a rancher they might hire on with, even if it meant riding uncomfortably close to Tucson, since Curry had found nothing in the El Paso area.

Kid Curry sat smiling, his thoughts on the blonde, sighing. 'I wonder where she is, if she went back to St Louis . . . '

Hannibal Heyes was reading the last page. His hands tightened, crumpled the edges of the folded sheet and his body rose from the seat, stiffening as though rigor mortis was taking hold.

'Curry,' The word choked out. 'She's right here. Read this.'

He did not pass the paper over. It seemed glued to his fingers. Kid Curry had to step behind him and crane over his shoulder. In a box at the lower corner framed in a scroll border was a modest message.

Miss Angela Christian and Mr Emile Chavez announce their marriage, performed on Tuesday last by the Reverend Endicott Peabody, rector of the Episcopal Church of Tombstone.

Neither of the partners breathed for a long minute while they read and reread, trying to change the meaning of the words. The cold print registered change. Hannibal Heyes at length pried his fingers open, let the paper drop silently.

Kid Curry rubbed at his throat, stretching his head to relieve the constriction of his breathing apparatus. He managed a whisper.

'I want a drink.'

'Costs money.'

'I want two. There's a dollar left.'

Heyes nodded slowly, turned, took Curry's elbow, pressed it once, let it go and they moved in stride through to the bar. With glasses in their hands they lifted them to each other.

Curry mused, 'For a man who moves like molasses in January he does make time. They stopped in Tombstone on the way north from Mexico. That trip cost us the whole works.'

'Uh-huh. Apache gold, she said. The price is pretty high.'

Westerns in Tandem editions

Action-packed novels featuring the Rio Kid by Tom Curry

Frontier Massacre 35p
Kansas Marshal 35p
Blood on the Plains 35p
Rampage of Terror 35p
Riders of Steel 35p
Valley of Death 35p

'Alias Smith & Jones' – new exploits by TV's most famous outlaws by Brian Fox

Dead Ringer 35p
Outlaw Trail 35p
Cabin Fever 40p
Apache Gold 40p

War Journey Fred Grove 35p
Sanaco Fred Grove 35p
The Trampling Herd Paul I. Wellman 40p
The Blazing Southwest Paul I. Wellman .. 40p
Big With Vengeance Cecil Snyder 30p
Fig Tree John Edwin Corle 35p

Gordon Landsborough

Battery From Hellfire

North Africa. The desert, June, 1942. Rommel battering his way through a reeling Allied army towards Alexandria. In his path a mobile ack-ack column, new to the desert . . .

'It has everything, knowledge of the desert and of mechanised war, supremely good characterisation, descriptive brilliance, and a 'special idea', masterly in its simplicity – a major's insistence, at the risk of mutiny, on saving a mobile gun.' *Birmingham Post*

40p

Patrol to Benghazi

A man-hunt in the Western Desert . . .
Hour after hour trucks of the Desert Patrol crawled in the heat of the dry African sun. Time after time the men had to clear the track, manhandling their heavy, laden lorries. Time after time they went wrong, running into impassable wadis or cliff faces. They were desperate men on a desperate mission behind the enemy lines – and one of them might be a traitor.

'. . . the background authentic, the adventure brilliantly imagined.'
Birmingham Post

40p

Long Run to Tobruk

From the heart of the Libyan desert the daring marauders struck, destroying Rommel's air fleet on the ground. But the S.A.S. could not be allowed to get away with it, and Rommel ordered them to be pursued, and killed or captured. So began one of the greatest man-hunts of the war – a small patrol of British guerillas hounded over the vast Sahara, doubling and turning in their tracks to throw off the relentless pursuers.

'Use any means,' ordered the Field-Marshal, and they did – flying columns. Stuka dive-bombers and even paratroops.

45p

Name ....

Address ....

Titles required ....

....

....

....

....

....

....

- - - - - - - - - - - - - - - - -